THE
KEEPER'S SIX

◉   ◉   ◉   ◉   ◉   ◉

Also by KATE ELLIOTT

Black Wolves
The Golden Key (with Melanie Rawn and Jennifer Roberson)
The Labyrinth Gate
The Very Best of Kate Elliott (collection)
Servant Mage

The Court of Fives Trilogy

Court of Fives
Poisoned Blade
Buried Heart

The Spiritwalker Trilogy

Cold Magic
Cold Fire
Cold Steel

The Crossroads Trilogy

Spirit Gate
Shadow Gate
Traitors' Gate

The Crown of Stars Series

King's Dragon
Prince of Dogs
The Burning Stone
Child of Flame
The Gathering Storm
In the Ruins
Crown of Stars

The Novels of the Jaran

Jaran
An Earthly Crown
His Conquering Sword
The Law of Becoming

The Highroad Trilogy

A Passage of Stars
Revolution's Shore
The Price of Ransom

The Sun Chronicles

Unconquerable Sun
Furious Heaven

THE
KEEPER'S SIX

⊙ ⊙ ⊙ ⊙ ⊙ ⊙

KATE ELLIOTT

TOR PUBLISHING GROUP
NEW YORK

TOR
DOT
COM

THE KEEPER'S SIX

A Tordotcom Book
Published by Tom Doherty Associates/Tor Publishing Group
120 Broadway
New York, NY 10271

www.tor.com

Tor® is a registered trademark of Macmillan Publishing Group, LLC.

Library of Congress Cataloging-in-Publication Data

Names: Elliott, Kate, 1958– author.
Title: The keeper's six / Kate Elliott.
Description: First Edition. | New York : Tordotcom, 2023. | "A Tom Doherty Associates Book."
Identifiers: LCCN 2022034340 (print) | LCCN 2022034341 (ebook) | ISBN 9781250769077 (hardcover) | ISBN 9781250769060 (ebook)
Subjects: LCGFT: Fantasy fiction. | Novels.
Classification: LCC PS3555.L5917 K44 2023 (print) | LCC PS3555.L5917 (ebook) | DDC 813'.54—dc23/eng/20220721
LC record available at https://lccn.loc.gov/2022034340
LC ebook record available at https://lccn.loc.gov/2022034341

Our books may be purchased in bulk for promotional, educational, or business use. Please contact your local bookseller or the Macmillan Corporate and Premium Sales Department at 1-800-221-7945, extension 5442, or by email at MacmillanSpecialMarkets@macmillan.com.

First Edition: 2023

Printed in the United States of America

0 9 8 7 6 5 4 3 2 1

To the families, large and small, found and
blood, who have each other's backs

THE
KEEPER'S SIX

◉　　◉　　◉　　◉　　◉　　◉

The call came at night.

Esther fumbled for the phone lying on the side table. Still barely conscious, she stuck it to her ear.

"Hello!" What time was it?

Static hissed and whistled.

Then:

"Mom, I need your help."

Her son's voice, tight with fear.

She sat up, heart racing, everything sharp: the book she'd fallen asleep reading pressed under her arm, the open jalousie windows, trade winds stirring the air inside the room.

"Daniel. Where are you? What do you need?"

". . . ruin . . ."

The connection cut off. Yet she could have sworn she heard an echo of high, sly laughter fading the way a train's whistle recedes.

Ruin.

Intimations of doom crowded into her head until she couldn't feel the phone in her hand.

A dog's distant bark shocked her out of her frozen state. The gold ring she wore on her thumb pressed so hard against her jaw it probably would raise a bruise. She lowered the phone to check the time: 2:22 A.M.

She checked to see the incoming number. There was no record of a call. She checked her text messages, her incoming calls again. Nothing. The last call registered was at 5:14 P.M. the previous day from an electrician about replacing the useless fluorescent fixture in the carport.

Nausea stirred in her stomach, an old fear reaction she'd worked diligently to train herself out of but Pavlov died hard. Reflexively she closed her hand around the Star of David she wore, using the action as a shield to calm herself. After releasing the necklace, she tapped in the "contact me" code to her daughter's emergency number. After kicking off the sheet she lit her way with the phone's screen to the closet, not wanting to turn on the house lights or even risk the brighter glow of the built-in flashlight. It was incredibly unlikely a Concilium picket was stationed outside watching for any sign she intended to violate her suspension, but it was always wisest to assume one was. The closet's tidy organization had come courtesy of Daniel's spouse, Kai, and included a drawer with dividers for her Hex gear so she could dress in the dark. A year had passed since she'd last opened the drawer, but the routine slid easily through her movements.

She dropped her nightclothes on the floor, pulled on underwear and wrestled into a sports bra with a flat pocket sewn into the side of each cup with the reassuring presence of a Keep key tucked inside. Wool socks. Utility pants with cargo pockets. A wool long-sleeve shirt and over it her faded travel vest with more pockets. It was all about pockets, and the pockets contained gloves, a collapsible hat, a multi-tool, a slim book, a small waterproof field notebook, a manual-wind watch, the Hex's badge, and four shiny gold rings.

Pono pushed up against her, moist nose bumping the back of her hand.

"Stay here, boy. Guard the house."

He whined softly. His neck tentacles unwound to hiss at the air as he followed her down the stairs. A full flask of water and a hip flask of whiskey always sat by the front door. She grabbed her boots from the lower right corner of the shoe rack, scratched Pono under his second chin, and went out through the carport into the side yard. Once, she could have vaulted the four-foot wall that separated her property from the neighbor's without thinking about it. Now, she jumped up to sit on the flat top, swung her legs over with a grunt, and hopped down into a crouch. Her left knee twinged.

All was silent in a neighborhood seemingly fast asleep. She shut her eyes and kicked her senses up one notch. It was like expanding her skin outward to feel the textures and temperatures as far as a line of sight. The "dark" form of her Lantern magic was passive; it allowed her to get a sense of life without illumination tripping alarms and waking people up. Her Hex had been suspended in disgrace a year ago, but that didn't mean the Concilium believed she and her crew were really on hiatus. Clans, enterprises, and cross-Realm trading and political leagues competed fiercely over resources and access, which meant a trained, functioning Hex was a precious resource.

Bugs. Anoles. A prowling rat. An exploring cat. A dog dozing half on the cusp of a waking bark. Venomous centipedes seethed in lightless crevices. But no pickets, or at least *probably* no pickets.

The spell woven into a Keeper's key only worked under an open sky. Rising, she fished out the key tucked into the left bra pocket and placed it in her mouth. Its hard shape pressed onto her tongue as saliva triggered the spell.

With an acrid burst of flavor, the key returned to the place it had been molded, taking her with it. She had never quite gotten used to the spike of cold followed immediately by a smell like dog breath, pungent, rather gross, and strangely reassuring. It was Daniel's special touch, how she knew the key was taking her to the Keep he was bound to.

Anyone looking would have seen a fizz in the air like bubbles frothing. Her body would start to fade, becoming translucent.

She vanished as the last bubble popped.

With a hiss of displaced air Esther reappeared miles away from where she had started. She stood in a graveled parking area in front of the living quarters of the Keep.

The humble plantation-style cottage was raised up off the ground on a post-and-pier foundation with a lanai—a covered porch—in front and in back. The lot was tucked away out of sight off a paved road ascending a leeward slope in the Ko'olau Mountains. Even in daylight she would barely have been able to identify the grassy lane that led through forest and bamboo past the main part of the extended family compound and on to the road. At night a heavy darkness swallowed the surroundings like an inky black cloak. Much of that weight was the magic that concealed the Keep from curious hikers who might wander down an unofficial trail looking for a route to the falls. The rest belonged to the Keep itself, whose footprint was pressed partly into Earth's soil and partly into the Beyond in a way that made it easy to overlook, as if it wasn't quite fully present.

The front door of the cottage was cracked ajar. She listened for signs of trespassers or intruders. The work-shed to her right was padlocked. One of the swings in the swing set creaked as if pushed by an invisible set of hands. Otherwise she heard nothing from the clearing that wrapped around to the back of the house except the delicate tremor of a spider's web stirring in the breeze and the respiration of leaves. The dogs hadn't come to investigate. That was definitely concerning.

Her phone said 2:33.

Daniel and Kai had replaced the old steps with a ramp for Uncle Joe's wheelchair. She walked up it to the lanai. A pair of wicker chairs faced the driveway, a shoe rack set between them. A ceramic mezuzah was fixed to the doorpost. The doormat glowed with a guard sigil woven through the fiber. The spell would recognize if a hostile presence arrived at the Keep, although as a warning spell it could do no more than alert the occupants. Esther paused on the mat to let the spell recognize her, then sent her senses into the compact three-room house.

Geckos. An enviable lack of bugs. Five breathing humanoid bodies where there should have been six.

She touched the mezuzah, kissed her finger, then probed the toe of her boot through the crack in the door. It eased open on silent hinges well oiled by Kai, who was always fixing things. The front room's twin curved sofas and big-screen television set athwart the corner had a staged look, perfectly cast with a braided rug and tasteful curtains. The computer table looked undisturbed, the laptop closed, the monitor off, and the modem lights solid green.

Normally she would have removed her boots on the lanai but she wasn't sure what she might need to do and how quickly she might need to do it, so she kept them on.

She paced softly across the front room to the corridor that opened in the center of the room's back wall. To the left lay a dining room dramatically inhabited by a large koa wood table and chairs, a bookshelf, and a huge apothecary's cabinet with sixty-four visible drawers and at least eight invisible ones. To her right, shoji doors screened off a sleeping room with tatami mats. One of the rice-paper-covered doors was slid aside enough for a person to squeeze through. She looked in, letting her Lantern magic ease into her eyes so she could see in the darkness.

Five bodies lay inside, breathing with the steady resolve of restful sleep. Kai was stretched out across the big futon with the four little ones curled tight along kwo/his back like flower buds ready to spring open at dawn. In sleep Kai's third eye gleamed as a silver oval against a dark forehead. Normally at night that eye stayed open but it too was shut, and kwo/he did not stir even when Esther gave a warning cough.

She licked her lips, gone dry. A hint of vanilla perfumed the air. This was spelled sleep. Vanilla was Daniel's signature scent. He'd poured the spell onto his own family, either deliberately or because he'd been forced to do so.

Still no sign of him. Yes, his immediate absence was worrying, but she knew how to walk herself through the options before she went full on alarm.

Keepers were bound to their Keeps. They rarely left the grounds and they rarely slept because, like lighthouses, their Keep-flames needed to stay on day and night as a beacon to travelers making their way through the Beyond's treacherous landscape. Most likely something unexpected had come up at the Keep's entrance and he wanted to avoid the children interrupting and in his haste had caught Kai in the spell also.

He had to be here.

She pushed open the back door onto the breezeway that linked the cottage to the Keep. Molasses and Babka sprawled on the rear lanai, fast asleep instead of eagerly about their night patrol. That had been a potent spell to have caught the dogs. He relied on them as fearless watchdogs. A flare of anxiety rocketed in her chest, and she took a moment to ruthlessly crush it down, pressing a hand to her chest to feel the necklace beneath the cloth.

Get all the information first.

The doors off the breezeway, leading to the toilet, the bath, and the storeroom, were shut. Past the lanai's comfortable patio furniture and its latticework railing rose a massive banyan tree.

A mesh of pillar-like aerial roots surrounded the original trunk, which now existed so deep within the tree's sprawling superstructure that it wasn't visible from the outermost reaches of the canopy. A raised walkway led through an opening formed by a pair of intertwined secondary trunks and ran beneath the canopy to the main trunk of the old tree. She took in a last breath of balmy air and walked in past the outer ring of foliage. Out of ordinary Earth and into the Keep, a place partly anchored in Earth and partly anchored in the Beyond.

The transition snapped through her flesh. Tropical air shifted into the nutty scent of something cooking. Lights were on as she walked into the front half of the Keep. This spacious semicircular chamber had been repurposed into a family room with tumbling mats, a toy chest, bookshelves, and a long table with benches. Beyond the table was a remodeled kitchen Daniel had fitted out with a chef's stove and a work island. Keepers needed hobbies to tide them over during the long hours and years they spent on duty, and he loved to cook. In fact, although the room was empty, one burner was lit beneath an unattended pot, a whisk stuck inside as if he'd not had time to take it out. A light brown sauce slowly darkened toward a brick color.

Where was he? How had he had time to call her and yet

not remove the whisk? Why had he put Kai to sleep instead of calling out to his spouse for help?

She gave the sauce a swirl, feeling bits thickening on the bottom. After setting the whisk on a spoon holder beside an open cookbook she went to the inner door and rolled it aside. The far side of the Keep was the other half of its bisected circle, which the family often jokingly referred to as Pier 99. A beautifully lathed wood railing marked off Daniel's office space with its desk, a reading nook and a worktable alcove, and a cot for resting. A curving staircase led up to the hostel attic where travelers could spend a night or two before heading onward, but she heard no sound and sensed no movement from up there.

The security room was closed with its triple locks all active; it was impossible for Daniel to lock himself inside. Most of the rest of the space was taken up with arrangements of tables and chairs for travelers waiting to get clearance or cargo. All empty. No luggage or packs in sight. No travelers in a state of arrival or departure. No visiting Hex taking a rest and meal break before heading out.

A rope barrier blocked access to the archway and its boundary, which was set exactly opposite the point where she had entered the Keep on the other side.

The wall-like boundary past which lay the Beyond was opaque, which meant Daniel was not in the Keep, not in the house, not on the lot, and not on the narrow ring of stable ground that surrounded the Keep in the Beyond. He wouldn't have walked into the Beyond because it was far too dangerous for a person alone, especially for a Keeper.

Fear stirred in her belly. She gave it five seconds to swell and then mentally wrapped it up into a visualized box and closed it.

Investigate first.

The room was dim, lit by a single night light. She brightened a hand and by its light scanned the paperwork scattered on Daniel's desk, the one place Kai wasn't allowed to tidy up. There was nothing unusual in the reports and requests and bulletins. According to the ledger, held open with two off-world agates, the last transaction had been twelve days ago. Earth was a minor trading post, of little interest within the greater network except for certain singular types of wood that grew only here, silk, miscellaneous rare treasures and unique Earth foodstuffs that appealed to collectors and gourmands, the noteworthy adaptability of humans to Hex work, and of course the illicit traffic in parrots. Of the Keeps on Earth, this one was the most isolated and least used of those she knew existed.

She went back into the kitchen. The sauce was beginning to burn at the bottom. Turning off the burner felt like defeat, a scalding to sear her heart into ash. She'd lost skirmishes in her time; lost cargo; lost colleagues and a friend and a spouse; had gotten her Hex suspended when the Concilium figured out she'd taken on a mission from the five triangles enterprise specifically in order to not carry it out. Right now none of that mattered compared to the safety of her children and grandchildren.

What had Daniel meant by saying *ruin*? He must have known he'd have only a moment to give her a clue.

A cough, a footstep, and Kai appeared through the veil as through a translucent curtain, all three eyes open in alarm.

"Esther? What . . . ? Why are you here?"

"Where's Daniel?"

Kai looked around the kitchen in confusion. At home,

at night, Kai made no effort to hide the unworldliness of a person not born of Earth. A coppery epidermis shimmered. Three silver bands like gleaming tattoos encircled each upper arm. Gill slits down the neck were usually mistaken for scars. Atop the head a flattened crest that, in company, a glamor passed off as a stylishly short mohawk. The third eye, in the center of the forehead and aligned perpendicular to the regular eyes, was actually the least remarkable thing about Kai.

"He was in the kitchen," Kai said. "He was going to make roux tonight for—"

"Roux?"

"It's a kind of sauce. It's a word in the language you say . . . français? French?"

"Roux. In the kitchen. Roux in . . . Ruin. That's my clever boy."

Adrenaline thrilled through her with the hope for the clue she needed. The answer she prayed for. She turned back to the stove, to the open cookbook with its recipe, which was indeed for roux. The sludge was congealing into an inedible mess. She unhooked an empty pot hanging from the pot rack and set it on the counter. A colander fit over the pot's lip. She upended the sauce pot to drain into it. And there it came, caught in the colander.

An oval dragon's scale, about an inch and a half in diameter. It was as thin as paper and as tough as diamond.

Her mind went blank. Her thoughts slammed to a shocked halt, that instant where you tried to turn back, to pretend you hadn't seen the terrible news you wished to unsee as if that would make it go away. But denial never made it go away.

She'd been down rough roads before. She'd trained for

emergencies. For the struggle. She knew how to do this. She took in a slow inhale followed by a slower exhale to calm herself.

In a hoarse voice she said, "Daniel's been kidnapped."

3

Kai's third eye blinked with a flash of rose-gold illumination. An answering spark of light gilded the scale like a glimpse of sunrise on a distant shore. "By a boss."

"That's right. By a boss." She rinsed off the scale and held it out.

Kai didn't touch it but kwos gill slits flickered as if measuring the scale with other senses. "Stone Kindred."

"Not Metal?"

"Definitely Stone."

"Can you tell anything else?"

"Not without touching it. It's best if I don't unless there's no other option."

"Do you have any idea who it is?"

"I don't. But the taste, the scent, of the scale is familiar."

"How do you mean?"

"It's been long enough I might be wrong but . . ."

She waited as Kai took several breaths, clearly unsettled and uneasy.

"The first group that took me was humanoid. They had no dragon association I could sense. They traded me to a Hex while we were still in the Realm where I was born."

"They traded you to the Hex that transported you through the Beyond."

"Yes. It's possible the Hex was in the employ of the boss whose scale this is. That could be why it seems familiar. The contact lingers."

"You told me the Hex gave no name. Is there anything you can recall that would help?"

Kai considered. "Their badge was like a cascade of discs. Falling coins, maybe. They're the ones who delivered me to . . . to that . . . the chamber where . . ." The rest of the words died unspoken. Kai's third eye shut as if kwo couldn't bear to look into the past.

"I understand." Esther wasn't one to swear but she considered a few expletives before deciding swearing wouldn't help. "An unlikely coincidence. Definitely bad. Don't leave the Keep. You and the babies are protected here. I put in a call to Chava. There's no telling if she'll be able to answer, but meanwhile don't let the family know, not yet."

"But Esther—"

"Uncle Joe will wheel his chair right into the Beyond if he hears Daniel is missing. You know he will."

"Fo' shua." It was Uncle Joe's second favorite thing to say, after bumbai.

"Let me handle this. Nobody kills a Keeper. This is likely a ransom situation. I have some experience negotiating, as you may recall."

"You're a fucking legend, Esther," said Kai with the charming half smile that could literally enchant monsters. The smile vanished as the whisk tipped sideways and rolled off the counter, hitting the floor with a splatter of dark brown sauce like old blood. This was one mess that wasn't going to be cleaned up easily or without pain. The old grief hit her like a stab to the chest, but she accepted the hit and kept moving.

"I have to call in the rest of the Hex. You better meet them at the front door."

"Got it." Kai vanished back past the veil.

She pulled out the gold rings and starfished her left hand.

One ring was already on her thumb, for the Keeper of her home Keep.

She slipped a second ring on her index finger: Gate.

On her middle finger: Voice.

On her ring finger: Shotgun.

On her little finger: Ghost.

There was no sensation, no sense of contact. The magic didn't work like that. Hexes were a six-sided spell, except the sides were people. Each member of a Hex had a specific magic that allowed the Hex as a unit, anchored to their home Keep and its Keeper, to cross the ever-shifting wasteland called the Beyond. Someone had once compared the Beyond to the mortar between bricks, if bricks were material Realms like Earth and mortar was a trackless poisonous infinitely branching and changing dimension inhabited by ravenous monsters, venomous plants, and clouds of amnesia- or psychosis-inducing bugs commonly called antics. Passing through the Beyond was the only way to cross between Realms with trade goods, envoys, travelers, or for more sinister reasons. In addition, within the shifting badlands of the Beyond one might occasionally track down the pearl-like beads called dragon tears which, if swallowed, could heal your most secret hurts, grant you a heightened store of intelligence, dexterity, charisma, or strength, or make you temporarily immune to the Beyond's lethal dangers. Or so the lore claimed. She'd yet to encounter a dragon tear.

While she waited, she opened the storage closet where their travel packs were stored and pulled them out one by one. As Keeper, Daniel kept the gear ready and up-to-date even during their suspension.

How angry would Gate still be? Would she even come?

After this difficult year would Voice greet her with the scathing sarcasm that could wither a field of flowers with one contemptuous speech?

Had Shotgun fully recovered—physically and mentally—from the injury she'd sustained on only her second passage through the Beyond?

Ghost would say nothing, just smile with a compassion Esther hadn't earned.

Indeed, the first one through the veil was the big man on his little cat feet. Not actual cat feet, of course. Like Esther, Faye, and Marianne, Gus was wholly human. But he moved with the lithe confidence of a person who knew how to land on his feet no matter how far the fall.

"Hey, Gus," she said, tentative because his disapproval would have flayed her. But he gave her his warm smile with a single uplifted eyebrow as a question.

She showed him the bronze scale. It was hard to speak the words aloud, as if silence might mean it wasn't true, but it was true and no matter how much she wished otherwise, that didn't change the object in her hand and the message it sent.

"Daniel's been kidnapped." Her voice was rasping and harsh, scraped by the tears of panic she was holding in. "No ransom demand yet but it will be coming."

He grasped her wrist, his strength reassuring.

Shotgun charged in just in time to hear the words. Faye was as petite as Augustus was big. She was wearing her signature long leather coat and carrying her staff, ready to fight, like every good Shotgun. The limp she'd had for months was gone, and her energy was dialed up to fierce as she gave first Gus and then Esther a greeting kiss to the cheek. After hopping up to sit on the butcher block island, she dangled her sleek red boots. She checked her watch.

"The others here yet?" she asked as if they'd last been all together forty-eight hours ago instead of eleven months and twenty-two days.

"Incoming," said Esther, feeling the approach of Marianne like a storm blowing in.

Gate arrived with a hand clutching the elbow of an apologetic-looking Kai, which made Marianne look like a possessive mother of the groom unwilling to see her precious child wasted on an undeserving mate. She gave Kai the twice-over with her green-eyed gaze. Designer contacts; her eyes were brown.

Kai had pulled on a muscle tee featuring crossed paddles and a pair of faded board shorts and was looking a lot more male than he had fifteen minutes ago; Marianne's influence, no doubt.

"So, Esther, your boy is still swimming with this pretty fish?" she said in her grating way. She couldn't pause to read the room, or Esther's expression, or maybe she did and this was how she intended to proceed.

Before Esther could figure out what to say without snapping, Faye tapped one end of her staff on the floor, sharp and loud.

"Marianne, you know perfectly well Daniel and Kai were married before our suspension. Or did you get too drunk at their wedding to remember? Because I know you were there. I was impressed by how much cheap beer you can put away."

Marianne's upper lip curled. "You're out of your depth

and way too new here to pike your stick into history you don't understand."

Faye exchanged a glance with Gus. His shoulder shrug convinced her to let it go.

"Aunty, so nice to see you after all this time," said Kai in a pleasant voice.

She let go of Kai's arm as if the words burned her. "I'm not old enough to be your aunt."

"And I'm not a pretty fish, yet here we are."

Marianne laughed curtly. "My apologies, Kai. The joke was uncalled-for. It's been one of those days."

Taking another step into the kitchen, she stopped short of the roux splatter with the grimace of a fastidious cleaner. Everything about her was curated and precise. Even her adventurer's clothing looked pressed and fashionable, straight out of an overpriced catalog. Fists on hips, she aimed a glare at Esther. "Well? I have more important places to be. This better be good."

Voice sailed in last of all, with her uncanny flair for the most dramatic entrance, an important skill for the Hex member whose linguistic skills were crucial when it came time to interact with the varied people and languages every Hex would encounter. Lydia wore an unbuttoned and garishly floral housecoat over a vest, trousers, and boots made of griffin leather. Her hair was braided and secured atop her head with a hair stick in the shape of a double ax.

"My bright star Esther. Consider how we parted." Lydia set hands on hips. "How you brought us all down with you. Ruined our prospects for future contracts for the course of the *ten-year ban* the Concilium imposed. You froze us out of the trade that supports our families, and assured us you'd do exactly the same thing again should it come to that."

"You can take the person out of the theater but you can't take the theater out of the person," said Faye with an appreciative laugh.

"I missed you too, little Shotgun." Her smile at Faye was genuine but it turned into a frown as the piercing gaze swung back to Esther.

"All your words are true," said Esther, undimmed by Lydia's accusatory glare. "I would do it again the same way, because the Concilium used our evidence to nail the five triangles boss and their entire criminal enterprise. I call that a good outcome."

"I call it a stunt that got us suspended," remarked Marianne. She stuck a finger into the congealed roux and tasted it. "Overcooked."

"What brings you to convene us at this ungodly hour of the night?" Lydia asked.

"The inconvenience is just like you," added Marianne. "No consideration for others."

Faye opened her mouth to pop off a reply. Everyone tensed. She glanced around, read their body language, and closed her lips with a curt sigh.

Esther held up the bronze scale. But her fear for her son lodged in her throat, and no explanation came out.

"Daniel's been kidnapped," Gus said, coming to her rescue.

His words gave her the moment she needed to swallow and regain her footing. She'd long ago learned how to talk when choked with dread. "I believe the kidnapping was meant to leave me in suspense until a ransom demand comes. But Daniel left us a clue."

"What a drag. Poor kid." Marianne fingered the gold ring on her thumb. The hostility didn't vanish from her expression but something like pity tempered her anger. "If a boss has taken him you'll never get him back. Not if some expansionist dragon clan is thinking to replace him with a new Keeper at this location."

"That is scarcely an appropriate reply," said Lydia. "Even for you, Marianne."

"I'm just telling it like it is. I can't help people who don't want to hear the truth."

Esther's heart hardened as it always did when people told her what she couldn't do and wouldn't be able to manage but only for her own good, of course of course. "We'll see how it goes, won't we, Mar? Bosses ought to have learned better than to tangle with me. I know our Hex separated under abrupt circumstances that harmed all of you, because of what I did without consulting any of you. This time I'm asking. I intend to get him back before the boss realizes we know who has him. Are you with me for this mission?"

"Rajah dat," said Gus with a firm nod.

"Daniel's our home Keeper. It's our duty to rescue him." Faye turned a challenging gaze on Marianne, crossing her arms as if to stop herself from slugging the other woman. "I can't believe you'd suggest we lie down and do nothing."

Marianne had a thousand-watt smirk. "Since I like Daniel a lot more than I've ever liked Esther, I'm not suggesting it. Which means I'm in, for this mission only. I'm not going to lie to any of you. I have a lucrative offer from a properly licensed Hex that needs a Gate."

"Do you, now?" murmured Lydia with an award-worthy side-eye. "Run by an expansionist dragon clan, perhaps?"

"Fuck you," said Marianne in a light, joking tone, but her mouth was tight.

"Oh, I see," put in Faye. "You'll cooperate because you

need Esther's signature as our current Hex leader to release you from the remainder of your contract."

"Think what you want. I am not the one who screwed you all over. Esther did that when she didn't consult with the rest of us about the plans she put in motion. So I don't get why you're all mad at me instead of at her. Anyway, I'm doing this for Daniel."

"Much appreciated," said Esther, managing an even tone. *Let her be angry. Whatever. All that matters is getting Daniel back.*

Lydia spread her arms wide like a speaker on an ancient stage inviting the audience in, and she had spoken on some very ancient West Asian stages across her many lifetimes. "Tiiiime's a-wasting."

Esther checked her phone: 2:57. She turned it off and put it in the closet, then stepped back so the others could do the same with their smartphones. They synchronized their manual watches, and each grabbed a personal travel backpack.

"Provisions." Kai opened a cupboard to reveal shelves lined with neatly sealed pouches of waybread. Kwo pulled out six pouches and handed them out.

Marianne accepted hers with an exaggerated quirk of her brows. "Generous of you to share since everyone knows dragons are hoarders."

Deadpan, Kai answered, "Not all dragons."

Faye winked at Kai and received a smile in answer, not full-bore enchanted but enough to make the room seem brighter and more hopeful.

"Well, actually," said Lydia while carefully tucking the waybread into her backpack, "hoarding is a term Western cultures use. A better description might be nesting. Or energy caching.

It's a means of feeding, by which I mean perpetuating their existence. Which I mention not to pontificate but because we'd do well to remember the difference, if you're about to do what I think you're about to do with that scale, Esther."

"I am about to do that."

Marianne shouldered her backpack with a look at Kai. "It seems awfully optimistic of you and Daniel to keep making the waybread after the Hex was suspended."

"I wouldn't feel comfortable without a sufficient store of waybread." Kai's smile had an edge so fine it could slice you open without your skin feeling the cut. "I don't just make the waybread for the Hex. It's a way to connect with all travelers. A hospitality. Reciprocity makes for a peaceful Keep."

"A truism you'd do well to ponder over, Marianne," Lydia remarked.

Marianne set her arms belligerently akimbo. "Spare me the lectures. It's not like you have family depending on you, is it, Lydia?"

"I daresay you know very little about what family I have. But I can see by Esther's fulminating eyebrows that she is about to scold us for this not being the time or the place."

"We need to get moving." Esther met Kai's golden gaze directly, always a bit dangerous even though Kai shielded the full force of those magical eyes. "I'll bring him home."

"I know you will."

Kai's trust caught in her throat like a shard that might tear her open from the inside out. Tears welled, so she turned away and walked to the other room to make sure no one saw her wipe them away. She had a reputation as a stone-cold hard-ass to live up to. And her son to rescue.

"Let's go."

4

Marianne pushed past Esther and strode into the other half of the Keep. She halted at the rope barrier and gestured impatiently for the others to join her. Faye took her place on Marianne's right while Esther stepped up to the left. Lydia positioned herself behind them.

Marianne unhooked the rope from the stand and moved forward to wait under the arch, which had no material door or barrier, just blankness—intangible, impassable. Like all Gates, Mar wore three dragon-bone bracelets on each arm. She touched her wrists together. The bracelets met with a ring, dissolving into shards. The slivers flew forward in uncanny unison to carve a tear in the blank barrier as swiftly as razors slicing through fabric. The edges of the tear burned bright like flame, peeling away to open a gap into a blizzard-like whiteout, past which they could see and hear nothing. Any of the four could have stepped through but they had no way of knowing what awaited on the other side.

Gus glided past. Esther hadn't even heard him coming up behind.

He stepped into the dense fog and vanished in a hiss of static laced with the rustling snap of ice cracking. The sound reminded her of the background noise she'd heard during

Daniel's call, the backwash of a transition between a material dimensional Realm like Earth and the chaotic Beyond. Marianne began to count under her breath.

The Keep itself didn't quite exist on Earth or in the Beyond, and so Esther always felt that, standing here, she had already begun her journey. She murmured the Tefilat HaDerech, the traveler's prayer. *Guide our footsteps toward peace, and make us reach our desired destination . . .*

Gus stepped back into view. His frown could sink ships.

"Full Pitch," he said in his best crisp retired-military delivery. "A cloud at about twenty-five meters to eight o'clock. Swarming."

"They're just swarming or swarming living creatures?" Faye asked.

"Hard for me to tell with no light but it's likely. Thought I heard singing."

"Singing," said Lydia in a deep and portentous voice. "Consciousness, art, defiance, the rich banquet the antics crave most."

"That's fabulous, then," said Marianne in a tone larded with sarcasm. Her forehead was damp from the effort of holding the gate open. "If they're eating someone else it will keep them busy so they don't attack us."

Lydia's scorn was powerful even when muted. "Not so *fabulous* for their targets."

"You know what I mean. We can't save every luckless sentient being, can we? How much time do you reckon for the scale to take effect?"

"One full minute," said Esther. "What do you think, Gus?"

Gus sighed with his usual resignation. He wouldn't be in danger, which made it harder for him to send others into bad situations. "It's a nasty cloud of antics, the stinging wasp kind. The swarm could dissipate in five minutes. Or it could come straight at us the instant we step through. Can't predict."

"I give this gate ten seconds more, so make up your damned minds," snapped Marianne.

Faye grinned with the sheer wild energy of a true Shotgun, never one to hesitate when a possible fight reared its glittering head. "Let's go slay some asshole wasps."

At a nod from Esther, Gus stepped backward through the veil and disappeared. Esther followed, feeling the familiar hit like walking into a curtain of melting ice. Its slippery substance coated her body as if to immobilize her. With her next step, the shivering frost of the veil pulled away to leave her in a hot, parching wind and a lightless cycle of pitch blackness that could not properly be called night since the Beyond did not have sun, moon, or stars and wasn't a rotating planet.

Gravel and sand crunched beneath her boots. The ground was solid this close to the Keep. The hooting of an antic swarm clamored in her ears, so loud and close she could barely perceive another sound rising beneath it.

Singing.

The melody was unfamiliar, the style unknown, the syllables no language she recognized. Condemned prisoners might sing with such defiance, steeling themselves for the end. Or maybe the song was a weapon meant to fight against the swarm. Music worked that way sometimes in the Beyond.

Faye's staff appeared as a throbbing blue line cutting through blackness although it was too dark to see Faye herself. Lydia's arrival came heralded by a vibrating hum building deep in the Voice's chest with a rich, red, magical glow.

That Marianne came through last of all Esther knew because the gate hissed shut with a spray of sparks. Embers spun around Marianne and coalesced to become shining bracelets that seemed to hang in midair on the forearms no one could see because it was too dark.

No time to waste.

"Cover your eyes," said Esther.

She lit.

A Lantern was neither hot nor materially present, but many things in the wasteland they called the Beyond weren't materially present and yet were nevertheless deadly. The brilliance flared as if she had exhaled it outward, expanding to about ten yards, which meant to the edge of the Keep's solid footprint. Past that, the aura faded into the blackness of the Beyond cycle called Pitch. Within the half dome of space lit by Esther's magic, they could see in all directions except into the ground.

They'd entered the Beyond through their home Keep many times so she needed only a glimpse to orient herself. On this side, the Keep appeared as a round two-story brick tower with no windows and one entrance, now closed and locked. The circle of stable ground around it was safe to stand on because of the anchoring properties of the Keep, in sharp contrast to the lethal instability of the rest of the Beyond.

A swarm of antics swept and swirled and spun in a vicious murmuration at the twilight periphery past which her light was overwhelmed by unrelieved darkness. No matter how many times she entered the Beyond, the sight of an antic cloud tightened its grip on her throat.

Antics were ugly, mean, and about twice as big as Earth wasps. Fortunately, the light hurt them. They darted away, the movement and flashing wings melding into the blackness beyond the gleaming aura of her light. As the antics fled, she and the others were able to see what the cloud had been swarming.

Six humanoids huddled on the ground about twenty-five meters away, more like shadows than people. The darkness seemed to be trying to absorb them, and maybe it was. The Beyond's dangers were impossible to fully catalog because they adapted and changed too swiftly.

Instead of melting away, the humanoids began dragging themselves and each other toward the light. Although some Keepers refused entry to their Keep without payment or official writ, a compassionate Keeper like Daniel could provide a temporary haven. Yet without Daniel in residence, Marianne could not open the gate back into the Keep. It killed Esther to see the other group's fight for survival, knowing the scale's magic could not convey them onward in company with her Hex.

The mocking antic laughter shifted direction and started getting louder. The cloud headed back toward the rich harvest of souls they'd briefly deserted. Their writhing movement spun out of the darkness, and the cloud descended again on the struggling, half-stunned people desperately trying to reach a safe harbor.

"Fuck this! Dammit!" Marianne's bracelets jangled as she shook her hands in frustration. "We can't leave them."

"Go," said Esther. "But I have to use this scale. You have one minute."

"Let's do it!" shouted Faye. She raced forward, spinning her staff. It whirled like a buzzsaw with a high-pitched shrill whine as it cut the air. It took her only a few seconds to reach the forward edge of the cloud. Her staff sliced through it, sending antics spinning in all directions.

Lydia let loose an ululation whose resonant power drove the mass of the swarm backward as on a wave. Marianne ran toward the people. Gus could do nothing but his job, keeping an eye out for more dangers, for other monsters and diverse perils that might spill out of the darkness.

Marianne reached the little group as Faye's staff swept the air clear around them. Nothing about their humanlike forms and features and the uniform-like blandness of their nondescript dress identified what Realm they might be from. From this distance it wasn't clear how many had retained their full psyche after the attack, but at least two seemed to be able to recognize Marianne's beckoning hand gesture toward the Keep and her tap on her chest to signal *There you may find safety*.

The scale was starting to burn in Esther's hand, activated by its presence in the Beyond. She popped it into her mouth. It was so big it gagged her a little so she held her breath to let her throat relax. The metallic flavor settled onto her tongue as sticky and stinging as freshly cooked syrup flavored with chili peppers and lemon.

As the scale dissolved on her tongue, a force like an outgoing tide tugged at her body, starting to pull her with it. But she couldn't speak to tell Marianne to hurry. She could only watch, mouth sealed shut by a magic that bound the Beyond to the Realms: objects want to return to their source.

Lydia shouted, "Get over quick! She's about to fall through."

Marianne and Faye came running as Lydia turned her voice to a gut-vibrating drone that confused the antics. Esther's feet began to melt into the ground and the world churned into a whirl of bronze-colored wheels like so many revolving eyes.

She fell through the turning wheels. Proximity and the gold rings pulled her companions with her, although all she could see of them was Marianne's gleaming bracelets, Faye's shining blue staff, a wisp of gracefully twisting Gus-shaped fog, and a bloodred stone afire in Lydia's throat.

The last she saw of Daniel's Keep was the first humanoid reaching the tower and discovering a brick ladder mortared onto the side. Kai's handiwork. The ladder led to a shelter built atop the Keep, a third floor that existed only in the Beyond where refugees and travelers might be able to survive until a closed Keep could be opened into its Realm.

5

Esther hit solid ground. She staggered forward and ended up landing on her knees, as if she'd been thrown off a merry-go-round. She steadied herself on her hands. It took a few moments for her body to accept it had come to rest.

As her gaze came back into focus she found herself staring past her braced hands through a floor as clear as glass. Beneath her lay what appeared to be a busy warehouse. As huge as a full city block, the space pulsed with frantic activity. Workers were hauling, pushing, stacking, and hurrying along aisles and catwalks. The vast chamber was lit by bumble hives, clots of golden beelike creatures who congregated into spheres. The buzzing globes hung above intersections or moved to where workers needed more light.

She blinked, still feeling dizzy. The view was too much to absorb all at once, even for someone accustomed to traveling to unearthly environs.

Finally she looked up and around herself. The wide passageway in which she knelt had smooth walls and a rounded ceiling with the glossy sheen of mother-of-pearl. The corridor curved out of sight in either direction. She could not shake an eerie sense that she stood in the whorl of a translucent shell as large as Aloha Stadium, set atop a massive warehouse.

No sign of her companions.

A shout rang out nearby, although no one in the warehouse looked upward. Heavy footsteps sounded at a march on her level, distant at first and coming closer. Striding around the upward curve, a group of six individuals converged on her. Closed helmets concealed their faces. Plate armor encased them, head to toe, concealing what manner of creature they might be beyond having two arms, two legs, a torso, and a head. They were stockier and thicker than most Earth humans. She would have identified them as Ek'en because of the horns sprouting through their helmets but the featureless face coverings had no holes for tusks, so they weren't Ek'en.

Each carried a poleax. As they surrounded her, they lowered the spiked tips of their weapons in a bristling ring with her at the center.

She raised both hands to show herself unarmed.

A bell rang, fading into silence. The six guards straightened up into two lines, set the butt ends of their weapons onto the floor, and stiffened as magic solidified them into statues.

"Esther Green, I presume." The voice was cool and lofty. A human-appearing man stood about ten feet away. She was absolutely sure he had not been there one second ago. He wore a charcoal-gray suit paired with a waistcoat and a patterned yellow tie. Sunglasses capped the fashionable ensemble.

"I see I have come to the right place," she said.

"The boss did not expect you quite so soon." His tone remained even and without any trace of emotion. But her guess had been right: Daniel had gotten hold of a scale and tossed it into the roux for her to find.

"I'm always happy to save bosses the trouble of sending out a ransom demand."

His mouth twitched, almost as if her words amused him, but all he said was "Your reputation precedes you. Although you're not quite what I expected."

"I never am," she replied. "Why do you lieutenants always wear sunglasses, even indoors?"

"Is this better?" He pulled them off.

Naturally he was good-looking, rather like an aging actor whose velvety brown eyes were made even more interesting by a distinguished pattern of crow's-feet. He'd have looked right at home in an Iranian film, or perhaps an Israeli TV show, she thought with sudden interest, wondering if he were Mizrahi, then internally scoffed at her own thoughts. *Enough, Esther.* She felt her whole age as she got to her feet with less grace than she would have liked while under the sort of critical observation meant to put her off balance. Within her line of sight she saw no one except the six statues, herself, and the man.

"Where is the rest of my Hex?"

"Right behind you," he said with a smile as dangerously smooth as butter.

There were always powerful magical currents awash inside any dragon fastness, whether here in the Beyond or in some Realm. As if a window had been opened, she heard the whisper of Gus's feet, Marianne swearing under her breath, Lydia's answering murmur in a language Esther didn't know, the triple tap of Faye's staff on the floor as a signal to Esther.

"I don't see them."

"No, you don't. They're in another part of the hoard, waiting for you."

He snapped his fingers, and the whispers vanished. She considered protesting but knew the lieutenant had no power to undo what the dragon had done. The boss of this hoard would not take kindly to her assertive arrival. It would make kwo feel challenged. Bosses hated feeling challenged, so this was a bit of jockeying to claim a negotiating position.

Fine. Two can play that game.

"And you are?" she asked.

"I am here to escort you to him." He indicated the upper inward turn of the whorl.

She set out with a strong stride, walking past the statues and then him so swiftly it took him a moment before he caught himself and turned to accompany her.

Silence was a good negotiating tool. She asked no questions, offered no small talk. The passageway ramped upward with a consistent sinister curve inward. The walls slowly narrowed toward the inevitable apex, where the boss would be waiting.

Occasionally she glanced down. The transparent floor had a trick of magnifying the scene far below. Now and again that trick of angle would bring her a close-up from within the warehouse of a sweating face creased with worry and exhaustion, or a rack holding slender ivory horns like angels' trumpets studded with gems, or a delicate latticework cage containing a six-winged beetle with an eye on every wing.

The curve and width of the whorl tightened, bringing them to a last acute bend. She wondered if she would even be able to stand upright in the apex as everything contracted at the top of the spiral.

The man cast a measuring glance at her, and she cast it right back at him.

"I like your tie," she said, and was pleased to see him break stride briefly and touch the tie, a smoky yellow color patterned into a cascade of discs. Falling coins, Kai had said. "The color goes perfectly with the charcoal gray of your suit. But I guess you already know that. I still don't get the sunglasses."

"Occupational hazard. As you'll discover in a moment."

Ah. A shard of information offered. She'd gotten her first crack.

They entered the apex of the shell, its umbilical heart. Instead of a tiny attic-like chamber they walked into a space that could have housed a rocket ship. It was far too big, more space inside than outside, a disorienting shift.

She shut her eyes, took in a breath, and opened them again. Two football fields could have sat side by side in her field of vision. Above, the shell rose up like a gargantuan chimney toward an uncooperative sky barely visible through a tiny opening that might as well have been a mile above.

The boss was curled in the center, wings furled, huge bronze head resting atop huge claws. His glimmering crest rose to an impressively spiky height. He filled half the space, lounging comfortably atop the warehouse beneath. His warehouse. His *hoard*.

Seeing her, he blinked lazily. His eyes were as big as mill wheels and she had a powerful hunch that the most perilous thing about this dragon who might swallow her in one gulp was to fall into the wheels that were his eyes.

"So here you are, Star of Evening," he said in a voice that wasn't too big or too small but alluringly just the very right size to reassure you he meant no harm as long as you cooperated fully with his wishes and demands. "Returned to the Beyond after you were suspended from the Hex network for . . . What was it, again?"

A glitter in the eyes. A single lash of the tail. Expecting her denial or protest.

She waited.

"Didn't you . . ." The boss loomed a little closer. ". . . *kill your spouse?*"

She flicked a hand to wave away the accusation. It no longer made her defensively angry to hear it even as grief still lodged a shard in her heart. "What do you want?"

"I was going to send Shahin for tea."

She glanced to her right to see how the man would react to being treated like a servant. He'd put his sunglasses back on.

"You like tea, do you not?" The dragon's voice had the soporific seep of a sleep spell.

She fixed her gaze at a point between the slow cosmological swirling of his eyes. "I meant, what do you want from *me*? You kidnapped my son."

He huffed out a wisp of steam. "I see there aren't to be any niceties, no polite greeting to warm the chill. How abrupt and rude. We were taught better back when I was young. In those days even humanoids valued civility. How far the Realms have fallen. Shall we start again?"

"You kidnapped my son. I'd call that abrupt and rude. Uncivil, even."

"Fine. We shall go on as you have begun."

She wondered if he would remark on how quickly she had arrived, but if he did, it would be admitting she'd surprised him.

"You are in possession of something of mine that I want back," said the dragon.

"The proper procedure would be to file a formal request through formal channels within the Concilium." She was always ready to jump out ahead of the conversation. In the complicated politics of the Concilium, the Realms, and the Beyond, it was often the only way to surprise people into revealing information they didn't want to give up. Let them think you knew something, even if you didn't know.

His claws tapped the floor as his gaze shifted evasively to Shahin, then back to her.

She added, "So here we are, at an impasse."

"You need only return my spawn to me."

"Your spawn?" The claim surprised her into a disbelieving laugh. "Who are you claiming as your spawn?"

"The young person who lives past the veil of the Keep."

This was troubling, if true. "Are you saying you kidnapped my son to serve as a hostage to exchange for . . . for Kai?"

"*Kai?* What is a kai?"

"Kai can't be your spawn. You're not from the same kindred."

"Clans can make alliances across kindred lines. Alliances spawn."

"First of all, I have it on good authority the six dragon kindreds are basically separate species and can't interbreed any more than separate humanoid species can interbreed. You are Stone Kindred. Kai is . . ." *Don't give up information!* "Kai is not."

"This ignorance about dragons is typical, Star of Evening. All that aside, the spawn belongs to me."

"Kai belongs to no one."

"You are wrong. I traded treasure for this Kai."

"So Kai is not in fact your spawn. Just an acquisition."

"Thus by the law of exchange the spawn became mine, part of my hoard."

"People are not objects to be possessed or valuables to be traded or hoarded." She glanced at the floor, at the workers below sweating at their endless hauling and stacking and moving. "None of us should belong to another, regardless of what those in power think is acceptable."

"You say that because you are not in power."

"You believe my views would be different if I were in power. Maybe you're right. Maybe power would corrupt my way of thinking. But that's a discussion in the abstract."

The dragon glowed like embers promising a bigger fire. His deep voice spun a silky lure for the unwary. "It's true you can never be one of us. But I could offer you more space at the table. More mastery. A window onto the outer workings of the Concilium. An opportunity to put events in motion instead of merely react to them."

"I'm not interested in being one of your lieutenants," she said.

The sunglasses hid Shahin's eyes from her scrutiny but they also hid him from the mesmerizing wheel of the dragon's gaze. His mouth, his jaw, his attractive cheekbones: none of these twitched as she spoke. His hands stayed relaxed at his side, so maybe he was content to be what he was or maybe he was too disciplined to reveal any glimpse of emotion or edge of discontent. No clues there.

She returned her attention to the boss. All the alarms ringing inside her had to be closed away as she turned on her cold bitch face. "All right. So now we know what you want. Yet I can't help but notice what a drastic step you've taken. Stealing a Keeper from his Keep! The Concilium has come down very hard in the past when Keepers have been harmed or killed. They do not like interchange between Realms being interfered with. A closed Keep hurts all of you dragons, not just humanoids."

"Your Realm is a minor trading post." His scorn had a whiff of sulfur.

"But Earth is still a trading post. It is still in the game. And there's nowhere else to get parrots."

A lick of flame shot from his nostrils as he let out an exasperated sigh. "*Parrots*. I don't traffic in parrots. I am a connoisseur of the last and the lost and the one of a kind. Not what is merely the mode of the moment."

The dragon's annoyance gave her the opening she'd been looking for, a tiny crack in its scales through which she might winkle the point of a knife. "Kai is one of a kind in the sense that any one of us is an individual unique to themselves. Let me ask again. What makes Kai so peculiarly valuable to you that you would take this kind of risk?"

The eyes whirled a fraction more slowly as if he was searching through a hoard of options for the best answer for his purpose. "You ask too many questions."

She let him see her amusement. Every boss she'd ever confronted got irritated if they thought a commonplace humanoid might be laughing at them. "Shall I make some guesses?"

"You shall not!" the dragon rumbled.

"Not your kindred. Not your clan. Not your spawn. Definitely not your lover."

Shahin coughed into his hand as if choking down a surprised laugh. She liked him better for being caught off guard.

"I could blast you into ashes!" The great shell trembled, an effective bit of intimidation.

"But you won't, because I'm your conduit to Kai."

"There are other Hexes operating out of your Realm. They could help me!"

"There are other Hexes and Keeps on Earth, it's true. But those Keeps are far from ours. None of them know where our home Keep is. They'd have a hard time locating it physically, not to mention getting anyone local to trust them. Even if they did find us, they'd have to figure out a way to transport a very uncooperative Kai across international borders to their home Keeps. Earth is *not* a Schedule Five or Six Realm, you know. We are only a Schedule Four. Not even our governments know about the Beyond. It's purely private operations at the moment. That status, may I remind you, is by Concilium decree. So that's what surprises me about your action. What would happen if the Concilium learned you kidnapped a Keeper? Just asking."

The tip of his long, spiky tail flicked sideways as if he wished to crush her with it. "Now I see how you got your reputation."

"If I know two things about dragons, it's that they truly dread being in debt, particularly to another dragon." She paused.

The dragon blinked once, twice, like metal curtains sliding up and down over its mill-wheel eyes. "That is one thing."

"Did I forget to mention the second thing?" she asked innocently. "You hate unfinished business, don't you? It's like a form of debt."

Shahin cleared his throat, looking away, a hand pressed to his lips.

She went on. "I can't assess the situation until you tell me what the situation is. It must be urgent for you to have kidnapped a Keeper."

A swell of heat wafted off the dragon's scaly epidermis. "Your son left me no choice."

"How so?"

"He refused to hand over the fugitive."

"Oh, I see. You tried to reach onto Earth through the Keep. But Daniel wouldn't let you, so you took him instead. You figured I would trade Kai for my own dearly beloved son."

"Am I wrong?"

"Yes, you're wrong. I'm not trading Kai for Daniel. I'm calling your bluff."

6

"My *bluff*!" A boom shook every part of the structure: the apex, the whorl, the warehouse below. All activity ceased as workers froze, staring around for any sign of what the noise portended. From their expressions of fear and dread, she guessed such noises normally signaled nothing good, or at least nothing good for them.

The dragon could easily kill her. Could have killed Daniel already and dangled his corpse in the air as a threat. But he hadn't.

She raised her gaze to the tufted brow above the dragon's bronze eyes. "What are all those workers doing down there? Is there any point to all that moving and sorting and stacking?"

Sparks of indignation spat from his spiky crest. "A hoard has to be *managed*!"

"I suppose it does." She thought over her options and what she'd learned. She was sure Kai was not this dragon's legally recognized spawn but she had no way to prove it, and pressing the point would antagonize him. "Let me make you an offer. To start with, I owe you nothing. I am not in debt to you in any way."

A debt challenge made to a dragon had to be answered by the dragon. "You are not in debt to me in any way."

"Perhaps the easiest solution to our conundrum is if I offer you something equivalent in exchange for returning my son to his Keep."

The dragon lifted his head, more with derision than hope. "Do you have any idea of the spawn's value?"

Did she? Probably not, because dragons never shared knowledge about themselves unless they had no choice. For example, no one had any idea where their home Realm was.

She said, "To me, Kai is priceless. So should any soul be, according to my moral and spiritual understanding of the universe. I sense that is not what you mean."

"If you don't know, then I am not about to give you the information, and certainly not for free. Meanwhile, your son is in danger."

The dragon could never know through what trials Esther had learned to keep her expression flat and her reactions calm. "Yes, yes, you want me to panic, but as I've already reminded you twice, there are repercussions for the death of a Keeper. If bosses or enterprises could do hostile take-overs whenever they wanted, the Concilium's hard bargains and trade pacts would be moot. The lines of trade and travel across the Beyond would be chaos. A veritable Wild West."

"'Wild west'?" asked Shahin.

"A figure of speech," said Esther with a nod of acknowledgment for his entry into the discussion. "A shorthand reference."

"So I had surmised, which is why I asked."

"Are you interested in language and history, Shahin?"

His expression brightened but he had no chance to speak. The dragon stirred, a tremor shivering through the domain it had hoarded into existence around it. "The Wild West is a figurative reference to a many-years-long frontier expansion, an aggressive migration and settlement, an invasion of one group of people into the territories of others. A lawless time, as such things go, filled with greed, violence, and exploitation. Manifest destiny, as creatures like to say as they eat up others for their supper."

Shahin looked away, hiding his expression.

"How did you know that?" Esther demanded with a laugh. "I thought you considered Earth a minor Realm."

A puff of steam escaped his slightly parted muzzle. "What I know belongs to me."

"How human of you. But I want to get back to this business of Keepers. If you kill Daniel, you'll be killing a Keeper."

"I hope you are not going to become tedious in repeating yourself."

"Of the six corners of a Hexagon, Keepers are the least common and thus the hardest to replace. They don't grow like weeds on the ground, you know. They don't fall like apples from trees."

"What is an *apple*?" he asked with a suspicious flick of his whiplike whiskers.

"You don't have any apples in your hoard?" She whistled. "Well. Huh. Okay."

The dragon twitched. She would place odds that within a week he'd have apples in his hoard, just so he knew he had some there.

Having sown seeds of distraction, she went back to the main event. "Are you prepared for the backlash if you kill a Keeper? Let me see. Some of the possible consequences could be losing part or all of your hoard. Would that include pieces of your memory? Qué lástima! Maybe you'd even lose this solid headland of ground you've so carefully grown to shelter yourself and all that you treasure. Centuries or even millennia of accretion, I'd guess. Shall I go on?"

Silence but for the bellows huff of the dragon's respiration and a whisper of sound from the constant movement in the warehouse, slower and then faster and then slower according to a cycle whose patterns she could not parse.

She stood between the proverbial rock and the hard place, an impasse the dragon was clearly reluctant to bridge. Pride? Honor? Greed? All plausible. But if she'd learned one thing from the disasters she'd survived, it was when to make the gamble that might break things loose.

"It would help me figure out a solution if you'd tell me what you need Kai for."

A spit of flame scraped the floor. Shahin took a hasty step back as sparks tumbled past like marbles. She held her ground but it wasn't easy to not flinch.

"I need not answer to a tiny and insignificant creature like you. Ridiculous."

She waited.

He scratched restlessly at the floor, huffed, twitched his big tail.

She waited.

"Furthermore, the details of my hoard and trading activities are none of your business. Return this Kai to the place you found kwo."

"That *I* found Kai?"

"How else could kwo have come into your Hex's Keep?"

Esther could think of multiple ways but her instincts told her to stay quiet and let the boss keep talking.

"You and I both know kwo is on Earth, so there is no point in pretending otherwise. As I just said, after you return this Kai to that place, I will alert the other party to pick kwo up there, as required by the original agreement. Once I receive confirmation the other party has received kwo, I will return your son to you."

Busted. Apparently, he'd received payment for Kai but not delivered. Regardless of whether it was his failure, the lack of exchange made him a dragon in debt to an unknown "other party." No wonder he was desperate. But she had to play this with innocence, not let him realize he'd given away his weak bargaining position.

She fixed her best ingenue eyes upon him. "There's a simple solution! I'll act as go-between. My Hex can carry whatever the payment was that you received for Kai to the place specified in the original agreement. We return what you received, you're back to the beginning, and no harm done. No need to get the Concilium involved."

An agitated rumble shook the solid foundation of the hoard. "Is this a distracting maneuver? Are you saying you can't return the spawn to the place you found kwo? That you're not capable of it? You have a reputation but it might be false gold."

"I *could* return Kai to where I found Kai," she agreed without agreeing that she *would* do it. She would never ever forget her first sight of Kai chained in that terrible space. "But to what boss, clan, or enterprise would I be delivering?"

"You don't need to know who. Just where."

In one way it was amusing, but the larger picture wasn't funny at all. The boss's liability, and the obligations and shame it imposed on him, made him more dangerous, not less. No one except her, Kai, and Daniel knew it was she who had literally broken Kai out of the chains. No one except her Hex had heard a ragged youth standing on a rubble-strewn street tell her kwo had no home to return to. Did they know of any safe haven that might offer shelter for a day or a year, enough time to figure out what to do? The youth had asked with such a genuine, fearful urgency that even Marianne hadn't objected when Esther had allowed kwo to accompany the Hex as their sixth, their Cargo. At the time none of them had known the humanoid-shaped person was a shape-shifted dragon, none but Kai, or they'd never have risked it. They'd returned to Earth, a minor trading post of little interest to the Concilium. For the boss to have figured out where Kai was, even if it had taken five years, meant others could uncover the trail too.

Kai had felt secure and accepted on the islands. Had fallen in love. Had made a home with Daniel and the extended household. Had given birth to four adorable children, which had startled all of them because quadruplets were definitely unusual, although Kai had explained it was a normal clutch size for dragons. Kai had often told her that for the first time since early childhood, kwo felt safe and loved.

She wasn't going to let dragon politics and boss power plays interfere with her family. Not now. Not ever.

"That's settled then," she said with forced cheer, as if they'd just enjoyed an evening's fine meal and finer liquors and were now the best of friends. Skate over the words she hadn't said and hope he was desperate enough to assume he was getting his way. He was a boss, after all. He expected compliance. She'd used expectations before to grease the wheels of her schemes. "Before I leave, I'll need to see my son."

"Why would I let you see him before you complete your task?"

"If I can't be sure he is alive, then why would I risk my Hex to help you? I made that mistake once before but not again, I assure you. Which reminds me." She took a step forward. "You know my name. I'll need yours. Because that's the second thing about dragons. Contracts once sealed must be fulfilled. Names are surety."

The dragon shifted like a hillside moving. He rose, and rose, and rose until his physical form seemed to fill the heavens, half the sky his eyes. She had to look at her boots or be swept into the hurricane of his gaze. The floor shimmered as waves of heat boiled off it although she did not burn into ash and she wasn't sure why.

Except that he needed her and her Hex. For now.

His voice boomed. "You may call me Zosfadal of the Fifth Clan of the Stone Kindred. Shahin will accompany you to make sure you do not cheat me. Begone."

7

"This way," said Shahin in a mild voice, as if he was so accustomed to standing in the blast zone of a dragon who could incinerate him that the threat no longer troubled him. Was he resigned? Apathetic? Cynical? Amused? Desperate? Impossible to know, but if he was tense, he hid it well.

He directed Esther not toward the passage whorl but to an alcove that opened onto an elevator, of all things.

"Where is the rest of my Hex?"

"They will meet you at the pylon."

"The pylon?"

"Is that the incorrect term? A gateway between what lies outside and what lies inside the encircling walls of the hoard."

It was clearly a bridge too far to ask that the Hex be allowed to accompany her to see Daniel. Anyway, the less time spent with Marianne the better, if Esther was being honest with herself. And she did try to be, as much as she could.

Shahin slid aside a grille door and then a beveled glass door, and they entered the elevator. Its polished wood panels, art deco suns resplendent with gilded rays, and a sparkling chandelier hanging overhead reminded her of vintage elevators in luxury buildings constructed in the early 1900s.

The control panel had only four polished brass buttons, arranged in a vertical line and with no number or letter labels. No emergency button either.

He closed the grille door, then the glass door. The suns glowed as the elevator began to descend.

"I don't see a floor-indicator dial. Is this a genuine antique elevator or a replica?"

"I'm not the encyclopedia you are looking for," he remarked, adjusting his sunglasses.

She grinned but he did not return it. And why should he be friendly? He had a job to do.

A bell rang. One of the buttons lit with a glow, although its shine faded as they continued to descend.

"This is for you." He offered her a bronze scale.

She plucked it out of his grip. "Does Zosfadal lose scales often? Careless of him."

"The boss will want you to return immediately to his hoard once the mission has been accomplished."

"Of course." She secured the scale in a vest pocket as a bell chimed again, a button lit and faded, and the descent continued. If the top button was the apex of the whorl and the second button was the entry level of the "shell," then they must be passing the warehouse level now, headed for whatever lay beneath.

When the lowest button brightened no bell rang. The sensation of motion ceased, which made her wonder, as she often did, about the physics of the Beyond.

She said, "When a dragon of the Stone Kindred creates solid ground in the Beyond for a hoard, does the stable area follow the laws of physics of the Beyond? Does it follow the physics of the Realm the dragon comes from? Or of some other Realm?"

He removed his sunglasses. Standing this close, she could see his eyes were brown and thickly lashed, a little too attractive and yet underlaid with the weariness of a person who has seen sights they'd rather have avoided. "The Beyond is an illusory world. The secrets of Heaven are hidden."

"By chance or by design?"

"You ask a lot of questions," he observed.

"I do what I can to illuminate obscure corners and darkling plains."

"I have heard the Concilium calls that trouble-making."

"Do you attend the proceedings of the Concilium? As Zosfadal's representative, perhaps? It's a task bosses' lieutenants sometimes take on, isn't it? Especially if a dragon is loath to leave its hoard, as they often are. Aren't dragons especially reluctant to leave a hoard that exists in the Beyond? For all they know some other boss might drop in unannounced while they're gone, intent on a takeover."

"As I said, your reputation precedes you." He slid open the glass door to reveal another grille door.

Past the accordion grille lay a cavern like the inside of a geode. The walls glittered with crystals of all colors. The floor bore the polished striations of banded agate. As Esther stepped from the elevator onto the ground she felt a sense of solidity, as if this deep structure was the true base of the hoard, the stable platform on which it floated atop the shifting nature of the Beyond like a continental shelf atop magma. An interesting analogy her daughter had proposed, back before she'd angrily departed the family business in the wake of her father's death.

Esther walked alongside Shahin into the cavern. The space was dimmer here, lit not by golden bumble hives but by the fragile flames of oil lamps and candle lanterns. People worked down here too although without the frantic moving and pushing and stacking that went on in the warehouse aisles above.

Clerks scratched at ledgers or read from lecterns. Fairylike sprites hovered midway up the towering walls wielding sparkling cloths to dust physical books and scrolls set on out-of-reach shelves. There were a lot of shelves and pigeonholes, a veritable library of tomes.

A portion of the vast space gleamed with banks of ovens, ranks of cooktops, and long steel counters where kitchen staff chopped, mixed, kneaded, and ground what seemed like rafts of foodstuffs. Daniel would feel right at home in such a place.

Shiveringly cold gusts of air alternated with warm, spice-drenched breezes. It was eerily quiet. Even the buzz of activity in the busy kitchen area seemed muffled, as if a blanket had been thrown over the entire space to smother noise.

Not a single clerk or sprite glanced their way as Shahin escorted Esther toward the center of the cavern, which lay in a darkness unrelieved by light. As they approached, a pathway lit beneath their feet to guide them into a standing henge made up of large golden cages ornamented like birdcages with filigree and jewels. Most of the cages were empty, thank goodness.

But three held captives. A metal-colored creature had curled up into a tight ball like a fantastical armadillo. A beast she thought at first glimpse was a lion turned out on closer inspection to be a chimera, with a second head slumbering against its tawny back and a snake's tail that stirred sluggishly as they passed, as if it no longer had the heart to fight. A humanoid clutched a cage's bars with four-fingered hands. This person had scaly skin, folded wings, and two humanlike amber eyes with two more eyelike bumps higher up on its hairless skull. A stark stare hit a dagger to her heart, as if accusing her of complicity in imprisonment, but the humanoid made no attempt to communicate that she could hear or feel.

They walked on, leaving the captives behind. She couldn't act now, but she'd write down a case log in her field notebook in the hope she could do something about the imprisoned, later.

Abruptly Shahin began walking faster, muttering under his breath. It was the first sign of naked emotion he'd shown so far. He halted in front of an empty cage whose door stood open. "Gaoler! Are you not on duty? The Keeper was placed in this container. He should be here, where I left him secured."

Harsh words gathered on her tongue. Daniel should never have been taken. The Keep should never have been breached. She wanted to lash out in frustrated, anxious anger. But she knew better. People used these sort of tactics all the time to upset and confound their opponents.

She spoke in as even a tone as she could manage. "So where is the Keeper now?"

Before Shahin could reply, a tall person loomed out of the dimness. Their height was made more formidable because they wore white armor and carried a spear and a ring of keys. The gaoler had the face of an angel, if by angel one meant a terrifying being with four faces. Fortunately a humanlike face was currently turned toward them, regarding them from its lofty seven-foot height.

"What?" the gaoler asked, none too pleased to see Shahin.

"Where is the prisoner? Has he escaped?"

"Everything is in order. No disturbances. No escapes. I was on my break."

"The workers here get breaks?" Esther asked Shahin.

"I'm not a supervisor, so I wouldn't know."

The gaoler examined her with more intensity. "Our terms of service say nothing about breaks being allowed. The Keeper said if there's no trouble we should be allowed to take a cup of coffee or bone broth and one of those delicious hot crescent pastries I was enjoying just now."

How like Daniel!

"Is it too much to ask for five minutes off our feet?" the gaoler added peevishly.

"The right to have breaks should be written into your term of service!" said Esther.

"We get no say in the terms we sign when we arrive here," said the gaoler, still with that steady stare.

"Typical of these bosses." She chanced a glance at Shahin, but he had hurried over to a tall, glass-fronted bookshelf and opened it to peer inside at ancient leather-bound volumes and fragile old ribbon-bound scrolls as if looking for Daniel amid the books. She lowered her voice and leaned toward the gaoler. "Perhaps you've heard of other conglomerations of workers who united together to demand labor rights and better working conditions?"

"Against bosses? That seems like a tale told to children."

She would have said more but Shahin shut the bookshelf's glass door.

He addressed the gaoler. "How can you say there's no trouble when the prisoner has escaped his cage? Perhaps with your connivance?"

Another being might have glanced guiltily in whatever

direction the escapee had taken, but the gaoler had four faces and need not move at all. "No one can escape the boss. You know that as well as the rest of us do, Poet. The cages are for show."

"Or cruelty," said Esther, earning her a sharper glance from the gaoler and then a second glance as it turned its head to allow its eagle face to examine her.

At that moment, Daniel's distinctive, hearty laugh rang out above the buzz of activity and was answered by surprised, scattered laughter. Such a strong wave of relief flooded her that it took a moment to catch her breath.

"What is he doing in the kitchen? Who let him out?" demanded Shahin, by now fully catapulted out of his cool above-it-all demeanor.

She often used humor to get hold of herself. "I wouldn't put odds on anyone trying to keep Daniel out of a kitchen where food prep is going on. Wild horses . . ." She raised a hand to get the attention of the gaoler, using her Lantern magic to give her fingers a soft, unthreatening gleam. "It's pretty dark here. Can you show me the best route over there? My thanks."

A simple thank-you opened many doors. The gaoler clopped away on sturdy legs that ended in stout bull hooves, a formidable weapon in their own right. She followed without waiting for Shahin's permission.

Past the outer edge of the henge of cages lay a wide avenue paved with mosaic. The images unfolded like a scroll telling a story. The pavement was Roman in its precision but depicted flora, fauna, and landscapes not at all Earthlike. She recognized the Realm of the Ek'en, which human Hexes called Ek'nyanyar. She'd not yet walked in that land, only encountered these ubiquitous allies of the dragon kindred in and about her travels. But someone from Earth had gotten there. Amid the mosaic's scenery there stood out a red-gold-and-blue-feathered parrot. The bird was elevated on a perch and seemed to be entertaining a crowd of horned and tusked notables garbed in flowing robes and in monumental hats adorned with horn ornaments that reminded her of jewel-hung cat's cradles.

The avenue brought them to a painted boundary stripe that marked out the outer edge of the kitchen area. The gaoler halted, unwilling to cross the line. She stepped over it into the steamy heat of a busy kitchen, quite a bit warmer than the chilly air elsewhere even though there was no apparent wall between the two.

At the outermost counters, youthful-looking humanoids washed pots and pans at big sinks while others were peeling what looked suspiciously like actual Earth potatoes. The youths glanced curiously at her, saw Shahin, and bent their heads back to work.

Esther headed straight toward a big table where a great deal of activity was swirling. At the center of it all stood a young man of medium height and heavyset build, his mass of curly hair and neatly trimmed beard framing an attractive face.

Yet it wasn't his pleasant features that brought people to cluster around him. It was the way he laughed, the way he listened, the way he brought people close. He liked people. He liked to feed them, to nourish them. He'd been that way even as a baby, almost belligerent as he'd insisted on sharing his saliva-smeared bit of half-gummed bread with whoever was closest.

He hadn't yet seen her so it was safe to give him a good looking over with a mother's critical eye. He was rolling up wedges of jam-smeared dough and shaping them into little crescents. As he worked, he chatted up a storm with a goat-headed person wearing a cook's apron and a pale wraith who would have been at home in a haunted barrow if barrows had bakers. Two tall elvish-looking beauties, one stout and one slender, watched over his shoulders as they disputed in the way of folk who have discovered a common obsession and are delighted to argue about it. A dozen sprites hovered overhead holding bright thimble lanterns, wings beating so swiftly they blurred.

Something alerted him. He glanced up and saw her. A spasm of relief passed across his amiable features, immediately squelched. With a dip of his chin and a swift double wink-like twitch of his right eye he let her know he was unhurt. His hands did not stop rolling out dough.

She put on a big, brassy voice as she strode forward. "Not this again, Daniel. These stealth rugelach workshops have got to stop."

"Never! Laminate, or go home." A grin lit his face. "Excuse the interruption, my friends. This is my mother, Esther Green."

"You said she would come," said Stout Elf in a tone of surprise.

"I believed him," riposted Slender Elf, "even if you did not."

"I didn't say I didn't believe him!"

"Hushhh!" hissed the wraith. "Be ressspectful."

Esther reached the opposite side of the table and braced her hands on it. "Daniel?"

A firm "Yes." Followed by "And?" His look meant Kai and the babies.

"All secure. I paged your sister."

His eyebrows spiked upward. "Fun for everyone."

"I wanted to be sure." As she spoke she was aware every eye was upon them. Shahin had alertly taken up a position at her elbow. He would certainly report every word of their conversation to the boss if Zosfadal wasn't already listening in. The magic present in hoards was yet another secret dragons kept to themselves. She swept her gaze around the crowd, nodding and smiling. "My thanks to all of you for taking such good care of my spawn."

Daniel rolled his eyes at the old "spawn" joke.

"Perhaps you might introduce me to all your new friends?"

The individuals stirred eagerly.

Shahin stepped forward. "That won't be necessary."

"I see." She nodded at each in turn anyway, scanning their disappointment and resignation. People liked to be seen and acknowledged. She turned her attention back to the counter. Eight trays of rugelach were ready for baking and eight trays of baked rugelach were stacked on a cooling rack nearby. "So. How long have you been here?"

"Twenty-two hours." Daniel indicated his flour-speckled wristwatch with its mechanical movement. "You?"

She checked her watch. "About two hours—"

"What's this? *What's this?*" A thundering voice broke over them. A tumultuously undulating cloud of ash descended from above, scattering the sprites. "Who said you could come into my kitchen uninvited?"

"It was you who asked me into the kitchen when I mentioned I had recipes to share," said Daniel without missing a beat as he tucked the last raw rugelach onto a tray.

The cloud solidified into a smoldering and mustachioed

chef with a pallid, ashy complexion and ash-blond hair topped by a dark blue cap. "I didn't mean *you*, Daniel. I invited *you*. I mean this . . . *interloper*."

"My mother? She came to check in on me. I hadn't written or called her recently."

A collective gasp arose from the individuals crowding around. Their numbers had tripled in the last few minutes and more were angling over to see what was going on.

The chef huffed and puffed. "Who gave you all permission to cease your labors? Get back to work!"

A whip couldn't have snapped harder than his tone. The kitchen burst into a hive of activity as its denizens scrambled back to their appointed places.

"Is there a break room where my son and I can talk in private?" Esther asked the chef.

"A *break room*? This is a kitchen, not a fainting lounge. This young person is a prisoner of the boss, not a feted guest."

"Does Zosfadal fete guests?" she asked. "He doesn't seem like the kind who has many friends. But I've been wrong before."

Shahin sighed.

The chef looked ready to scald. "You must go at once."

Shahin said, "You have assured yourself that your son is hale."

She caught Daniel's eye with her best meaningful look. "All right. Hold tight. I have some business to take care of."

"How unlike you, Mom," said Daniel with a straight face that normally meant he was laughing inside. But she knew him. He was anxious, probably more for his spouse and children than for himself. But for himself too. The kidnapping had been sudden and unexpected. Esther was certain she, her Hex, and Kai had fled the collapsing entrepôt that long-ago day without being traced. Otherwise she'd have been hauled before the Concilium on the most serious charge of a humanoid transporting a captive dragon. But it had been five years. Deeds did tend to catch up with people, especially when they went against the power of the status quo.

She slipped a hand into a cargo pocket and fished out the book she'd stashed there last year, before the Hex had been suspended from travel through the Beyond. She always kept an organizing book on hand. She slid it across the table to her son.

He picked it up before Shahin could react and tucked it into his apron's front pocket. "Really, Mom? *Rules for Radicals*? Can we get some twenty-first-century organizing literature here?"

"The first rule is that it has to fit in a cargo pants pocket."

"What is that? What manner of book?" Shahin asked.

She turned to look at him directly in the reflective sunglasses. "It's my book, not any part of Zosfadal's hoard, thus out of your jurisdiction. Shall we go?"

Daniel beckoned to the wraith, who lingered by one of the cooling racks. "Sshaiaia, might you kindly collect a dozen rugelach, and some of the savory rolls, if you wouldn't mind."

"My pleasssure," whispered the wraith with a shy smile.

The chef fulminated, voice cracking like an explosion. "Who are you to steal from the kitchen? All this debt will be entered on your ledger. I forbid any such trafficking—"

"Was it *you* who created the recipe for those excellent savory rolls, Chef?" Daniel interrupted smoothly.

"Of course it was me!"

"There's a spice flavoring them I've never tasted before. Do you know what Realm it comes from? Are they a trading Realm or an exploited one?"

The chef's form shed flakes of ash. "An exploited one? What do you mean, *exploited*?"

"You don't use that terminology here?" Daniel looked around as if inviting comments. Everyone had fled back to work, but they were listening. "I meant whether a Realm is a knowing partner with the Concilium trading network or is a place Hexes come and go in secrecy taking what they wish for the profit of outsiders."

The wraith glided soundlessly over and thrust a small fabric bag into Esther's hands, then pointed toward the walls with its narrow chin as if to say *Escape now while you still can.*

Esther nodded her thanks and hurried after Shahin.

8

"Incredible," muttered Shahin as he led Esther out of the kitchen into the darker half of the cavern. Did he know he had a profile that handsomely displayed his deep-set eyes, aquiline nose, craggy chin, and designer-level five-o'clock shadow? A long-buried flicker of attraction lit, the old dance of being captivated by a feeling, a face, a physical magnetism, by the lure of what might be if you just extended an opening. But she stamped it down ruthlessly. She had no time for distractions, especially not toward a boss's lieutenant who wore an alluring sense of mystery as well as he wore his expensive suit.

"What is incredible?" she asked instead.

"Many things are incredible," he said in the tone of a person changing the subject. He walked a dozen steps before adding, "And there is no time to discuss matters of incredulity since we need to travel immediately to fulfill the agreement. I'm given to understand the Beyond is not a place with shops or foraging. If you and your Hex wish to purchase provisions, I can take you to the warehouse store."

"The warehouse store! Who do they sell to? There can't be many tourists."

"The workers."

"Does Zosfadal pay his workers? That's not common among dragon bosses."

"Of course he pays his workers. He pays them with life. They are all people who would not be alive if not for him. They repay him with their labor."

"Ah, so it's a company store."

"A company store," he said, cleverly making it a statement instead of a question.

"A company store is owned by the employer and usually sells only to its employees at inflated prices. Often the store uses credit as a means to keep employees indebted to the company. In this case, with no other option for purchases, I might venture to guess those who live and work in this hoard keep sinking further into the boss's debt. Which makes their tenure here a lifetime arrangement, no doubt. You as well?"

"An interesting question," he said as they reached a tall wire fence. "This way."

He opened its gate and indicated an empty omnibus with a canvas roof. The vehicle had no driver, no horses, no obvious means of locomotion. They took their places on hard wooden seats. Shahin spoke words in a language she did not know and the vehicle began to move. It followed a stony band in the rock like a hardened river of orange-gold and was soon racing along at a fast clip, wheels clicking *ka-chunk ka-chunk ka-chank* as on railroad tracks.

Still inside the giant whorl, they rolled past fields and orchards where unknown crops grew. She could not see what they were and there was no obvious identifying smell. The chilly air of the street had warmed at the fence to become a drowsy midsummer night's humidity. How did crops grow here without sun? Briefly the omnibus crossed beneath a cloudburst hammering atop the roof canvas, if rainstorms could fall within tightly proscribed invisible boundaries. Then they emerged into rainless silence.

Fifteen minutes passed before the omnibus slowed and stopped. She clambered down to face a brick wall where a gate opened into a built-up area, ranks of what appeared to be two-story storehouses and barracks set in a grid pattern, streets splitting off at right angles. Here and there storefronts opened onto dimly lit spaces where people ate at long tables. Any murmur of conversation was low, as if no one wanted to be heard. Now and again a head moved to look their way, that was all. A pleasant tang of smoke permeated everything, and she thought it was not the smell of cooking fires but the presence of the dragon. Flowers had scent, and so did dragons, so she'd been told. Kai had been able to identify the bronze scale as Stone Kindred from a smell too subtle for human senses.

Thinking of Kai and Daniel and the babies stiffened her jaw and strengthened her heart. She'd make this gamble work. Somehow. Even if she was currently just buying time and space to figure out a plan. To collect more information. To find a fatal crack in Zosfadal's scaly hide.

She said, "This is a gloomy place. Aren't there community halls or cafés? Gymnasiums or theaters? Skate parks or swimming pools? Places people can congregate and relax besides those grim cafeterias?"

Shahin's shoulders twitched as he suppressed a reaction. He said, "You can ask the boss if we return."

"An interesting way to phrase it. Do you have some reason to think we might not return?"

"All manner of people disappear into the Beyond and are never found again."

He had timed his comment well. They approached the cliff-like wall of the cavern with its crystalline edges. It rose up into utter darkness except for a pair of lights skittering far above that might have been a pair of sprites going about their duties. It occurred to Esther that sound and light in this cavern did not persist across distance in normal ways. Even if the dragon provided a stable platform on the inconstant and often intangible sands of the Beyond, the hoard still lay in the Beyond and not in a Realm.

"What do *you* think the Beyond is?" she asked. "You must have a theory. Everyone else does."

Shahin said, "'Wandering between two worlds, one dead, the other powerless to be born.'"

"I'm sure I've heard that before. Is that Yeats? No, it's Matthew Arnold, isn't it? I quoted him earlier. The 'darkling plain.' How do you know Matthew Arnold's poetry?" She blinked as memory stirred. She'd been so eager to find Daniel she'd missed a clue. "Didn't the gaoler call you a poet?"

"Here we are." He halted at a bronze-plated door set into the wall and surrounded by a bristling ring of spiky crystal growths. "This is your chance to change your mind about whatever it is you're planning. I hear how carefully you phrase your words. It would be easier for everyone concerned if you simply returned the spawn, as the boss suggests."

She snorted. "Easier for the boss, you mean. No thanks. Let's go."

The door looked heavy but opened as if on ball bearings to reveal a tunnel hewn through the rock. They started walking, Esther checking her watch to time the distance as she counted steps. The tunnel was about a mile long and had been divided into shorter segments through the use of portcullises, all currently raised, and three chasms bridged by retractable piers. Zosfadal wasn't taking any chances with attack. Or escape.

The tunnel ended at a large gate banded with iron, guarded by two large individuals whose faces were hidden by closed helmets with slits for eyes. One of the guards opened a pedestrian door set into the left gate. Esther and Shahin crossed the threshold onto a cave-like terrace about the size and shape of a baseball field. The cave mouth opened onto a view of the Beyond, a hazy twilight smear seen in the distance. A freestanding pylon made of two pillars rose at the "centerfield" rim of the cave mouth. This pylon served as an entrance onto and off of the hoard's stable ground although there was no outer wall or railing. A masked person dressed like a medieval jester with particolored sleeves, a motley robe, and a belled cap stood at the pillared gate. The jester looked their way and shook a marotte in their direction as if in salute.

"That one," muttered Shahin with a frown.

When Esther glanced at him to reply, she realized he was talking to himself.

Here, at the back of the terrace, the only light came from two glowing spheres set on iron tripods on either side of an imposing desk. A grumpy-looking person spoke into the receiver of a phone that looked as if it had been reclaimed from the same old-fashioned hotel as the elevator.

"No. No. No? No! And definitely not." The clerk wore a double-breasted suit and looked human enough except for their compound eyes and a pair of antennae twitching atop their head. They slammed down the phone and looked up.

"Poet!" they called harshly. "You are to take the rucksack."

Shahin picked up a rucksack slumped against the desk. He picked through its contents, removing several wax-paper-wrapped items. "Take these off my account. I did not request them."

"You don't intend to eat?" demanded the clerk.

"I'll make do." He removed a bundle of clothing, sighed as he glanced around as if looking for a place he might change, then shoved the bundle back into the rucksack, which he swung over the shoulder of his expensive suit. "This way. Your Hex awaits you at the outer barrier."

They passed about twenty individuals waiting in a line, most huddled together in groups of five or six, some sleeping, all ragged and worn out. There were no fires, no heat, and the air was freezing.

"Who are they?" she asked.

"Applicants."

"Applicants? Oh, I see. Realm-born people seeking safe haven. In exchange for work. It's starting to make sense now. That was food from the company store you refused because to accept it would mean a debit against your account. I don't know how boss lieutenants function within dragon society. Are you employees? Serfs? Stakeholders? Prisoners?"

His jaw tensed. "Do you know what happens to people who ask too many questions?"

"Not yet!"

He touched his yellow tie.

When he didn't speak, she added, "You can ask no questions and still end up tossed onto the pyre. I know which road I choose."

He gave her a look she could not interpret. Was he about to answer?

"Esther! Over here!" Lydia's voice was audible anywhere, at whatever volume, if she chose it to be.

The Hex waited at the terrace's edge, seated on a set of benches placed for viewing the Beyond. Although the air on the terrace was cold, no wind blew in from outside. A shimmering veil like a magical force field curtained the terrace's open side. Similar magic shielded other hoards and entrepôts. A glass-like sphere enveloped the Concilium's meeting nest in the Beyond. Such "veils" allowed people to see onto the Beyond while preventing antic clouds and other dangers from invading. Even though antics could not hold their form for long once they flew inside the weight of stable ground, they could do a lot of damage before their inevitable disintegration.

Lydia, Faye, and a solidly physical Gus got to their feet, tense and anxious. Marianne remained mulishly seated as she gave Shahin a long up-and-down in her intrusive way, making sure everyone knew she was doing it, including him.

"He's here, and he's okay," said Esther as they came up.

Everyone relaxed slightly.

Marianne got her breath back first. "So what terrible plan did you come up with? I mean, since Danny isn't with you, I guess you couldn't just magically spring him. You know, Esther, if you'd let us accept that other Hex arrangement when it was offered—"

"This isn't the time, Mar," said Esther. "Anyway, you and Trey were outvoted."

"I was outvoted. Trey was drunk. There's a difference." Marianne stood, arms crossed. "You need me, so don't piss me off."

Exasperation sang in Esther's bones. How she wanted to snap! She forcefully reminded herself of how Daniel made the best of things in the worst situation. For example, kidnapped and clapped into a cage, yet he found ways to make allies. For example, five years ago when she'd brought home a battered, exhausted, nerve-wracked, and nightmare-ridden refugee, the others had seen only one of her pointless quixotic quests doomed to failure, a dangerous alien with no known history and no reason to trust—except Daniel, who always said he had fallen in love at first sight. He had the gift of seeing to the heart. He had the integrity and the patience to let Kai heal before asking anything more than Kai at first could have given. Kai could have said no, and kwo had known it before saying yes.

"Well?" Marianne dragged out the word like a taunt. "Cat got your tongue?"

"We can discuss this in a safer place than a hoard." With Shahin listening she had to be precise in what she said to avoid revealing any information to the boss that she didn't yet want him to know, like Daniel's relationship to Kai. She wasn't even sure Zosfadal knew exactly where she'd discovered Kai, and she hadn't been about to ask. "I need information in order to proceed, so we'll start at Dunkirk."

"Oh my," said Lydia. "I fear I see where this is going."

Gus rubbed his eyes wearily. He wasn't eager to return to the place they called Dunkirk, and who could blame him? Yet of all of them, once in the Beyond he'd be physically safest because he would again revert to a visible but immaterial form.

Faye said, "Dunkirk? Like the town in France? Like World War Two?"

Marianne narrowed her eyes, looking way too much like an ambitious accountant tallying up the latest haul. "I thought this was going to be a one-stop-and-done operation. Since it isn't, I proceed with the understanding this will be my last mission with this Hex."

Esther exchanged a questioning glance with Lydia. Marianne's capitulation to a longer Beyond journey seemed awfully easy. The Gate wasn't a sentimentalist even if she did like Daniel. Hex members got out as fast as they could if they distrusted their Keeper, but at the same time, Hex members rarely left a Keeper as reliable as Daniel. Which made Esther wonder about the offer Marianne had gotten. For now it didn't matter. This was the only path forward. She wasn't giving up Kai, and Daniel would never accept it if she did. They'd been down that road with his father ten years ago and look where that had gotten them.

No sense in beating a dead horse.

Putting on an actor's smile, Lydia gestured toward the view, a landscape seen as through lightening mist toward a blue-smoke horizon. "The Beyond awaits!"

"He's coming with us? In that tailored suit?" Mar flapped a hand toward Shahin.

"Ah, yes, forgive me. This is Shahin, Zosfadal's lieutenant. He'll be accompanying us."

Lydia swept an arm operatically to include the entire group. "Shahin, let me introduce you to the Hex. Excuse our informal manners. Augustus Ho is our Ghost. Faye Bi our Shotgun."

Faye gave a perfect curtsey ornamented with her sweetest sly grin.

"Shotgun?" For once, Shahin forgot himself enough to ask a question, although that could have been the influence of the Voice.

"You might say Sword or Spear or Ax," said Lydia.

"Ah. Shamshir."

"Persian, eh? Old school, I see. Well met." Lydia gave an elaborate bow. "You may call me Lydia Izmirli. I am the Hex's Voice. Marianne Sato, our Gate. Esther Green, our Lantern, you know. I assume you are already acquainted with our Keeper, so rudely bundled away to this lonely mountain."

He gave a polite bow of acknowledgment to the group. "The honor is mine."

"Nice sunglasses," said Marianne. "They look almost as

expensive as that suit. Are those shoes from Italy? A shame to scuff them."

"We should get started while we still have Gloam," said Esther.

Marianne shot her a look meant to provoke. "For someone who doesn't like bosses, you sure are bossy."

Esther had a long fuse, she really did, but she took a step into Marianne's personal space and set a hand on her shoulder, fixing her gaze. "Listen. It's my son, not just my Keeper. That's ground me down to my last nerve. The sooner we finish, the sooner you can be released from your contract and go on your merry way with whatever money-grubbing new partners you've found. Get it?"

Daniel and his sister would have gamely chorused "Got it" and she'd have finished with "Good," but it was the wrong time and the wrong place and the wrong relationship.

Marianne shook off Esther's hand and strode over to the pillars. The rest grabbed their packs and hustled after.

As a Gate, Marianne could easily have sliced an opening in the veil. However, within a hoard controlled by a boss, such an act was out of bounds. So many Realms and species interacted in the Beyond that agreed-upon courtesies and customs mattered, not to enforce behavior but to smooth out chasms of misunderstanding.

Shahin handed what looked like a coin to the jester, who used a dragon-headed scepter to part the veil.

"Safe journeys! Don't trip!" the jester cackled. "Hope to see you again, if you survive."

9

They passed from the chilly terrace into a dry, stifling stillness typical of Gloam in the Beyond. Gus took point. Marianne walked behind him with Faye at her right side. Lydia came next, then Esther at the back beside Shahin. A long stone ramp linked the terrace to the ground below, although the Beyond didn't strictly have "ground." They started down as another group emerged out of the twilight haze and headed up.

Faye began to bounce a little in her walk, excited to see another Hex and one clearly not Earth-based. Hard to fault her; this was only her third trip into the Beyond. Esther wanted to remind her to be cautious, but Faye had passed her training with flying colors and the injury she'd suffered hadn't been worse because of her swift reaction. She was as prepared as anyone could be. It wasn't at all odd for her to stare in astonishment, to grin as a child would, filled with glee. In retrospect, Marianne's lack of awe and delight for the miraculously strange existence of uncounted dimensions with their bizarre and ordinary landscapes and peoples should have been a red flag. Proceed cautiously with people who can no longer be bowled over by wonder.

Esther pressed her lips together and let Faye bounce

because, the truth was, Esther was excited too. She'd never gotten over the utter amazement that she could travel to other worlds and encounter such a rich tapestry of existence. If she survived.

The unknown Hex climbing the ramp wore badges with the same gold coin pattern on Shahin's tie. The Hex individuals were easy to describe in fanciful Earth-based terms as an ogre, a centaur, a stately individual with slowly undulating cilia for hair, a translucent Ghost whose contours were too faint to make out, and a handsome reptilian with a roguish wink for Faye as they passed, answered with a grin and a wink from Faye.

But among the Hex shuffled a pain-pinched prisoner, wrists shackled and broad back bowed under an apothecary's chest almost as big as the hapless person forced to carry it. The chest was doubtless filled with valuable treasures. Valuables like a Kai, perhaps, who had price or importance enough to make such an individual a worthwhile trade or ransom. It could even be a Keeper like Daniel, maybe one intended to replace Daniel as a way to blackmail Esther and her Hex into cooperation.

Keepers were both rare and precious. Unscrupulous enterprises and Realm-based leagues as well as freelance Hexes had been known on occasion to trade unwilling Keepers. Because Keepers were usually humanoid, not dragons, the Concilium might disapprove of and sometimes punish interference with them, but as long as traffic and trade weren't disrupted the dragon council might equally choose to not intervene. Imprisoned in a Keep far distant from their home Realm, such Keepers might never be found or rescued. The thought of Daniel's and Kai's vulnerability burst through Esther with a monstrous anger. She cast a final look over her shoulder at the ascending Hex. The prisoner hauling the cargo never looked up, as if hope had long fled.

"Are you all right?" Shahin asked, eyes still hidden behind his sunglasses.

She tapped her mouth to mime silence as they reached the bottom of the ramp. Gus walked into the Beyond, a transition made obvious by his abrupt transformation from someone solid to his Ghost form, both mute and intangible. He began cutting a zigzag pattern to check for traps and other dangers. The rest halted at the rim of the stone as Marianne stepped onto the gritty ground, knelt, and set both hands, palms down, against the dirt. Gates could open a tear in the veils between the Realms and the Beyond, and they were also pathfinders who could read finely grained differences in the shifting Beyond. They could sense oases. They could feel the weight of dragon hoards, the constructed fixity of entrepôts and peninsulas, and the all-important homing signal of Keeps.

Marianne stood and stepped back onto the ramp.

In a whisper she said, "The speed of a dragon scale spoils a person. We've got a long slog ahead. There two oases, one about two hours' walk, the other within a five- to seven-hour journey. Nothing else nearby. I say take the closer and reassess."

Esther nodded. Marianne might have her eye on the money but she was an excellent Gate. With Gus's and Lydia's concurrence, Esther had signed her on the very day the real estate agent had discovered an isolated compound she shouldn't have been able to find. She'd said a hunch had tugged her down a grassy lane that wasn't marked on any map, so she had explored it, hoping to find an undiscovered listing treasure she could profit from. She had found the Keep instead. Her sharp instincts, and an unerring nose for a thing she couldn't yet have known about, had led her to a transition spot between Realm and Beyond.

They set out, Marianne in the lead. Gloam was the twilight calm between the cycles of Pitch and Bright, which made it the best time to travel, if a Hex had a choice, which they usually did not. There were fewer deadly swarms and noxious monsters and enough visibility that Gus could range farther away and more easily direct them with hand signals around danger spots and impassable zones. Shahin's lips were moving with silent words. For a moment Esther could have sworn he was speaking in Hebrew. Praying the Tefilat HaDerech? Surely not. She wasn't a lip reader and she was probably just seeing what wasn't there. How likely was it, really, that an older Jewish man of mysterious origins had somehow become a boss's lieutenant in a hoard in the middle of the Beyond? *Let it go, Esther. Let it go.*

They fell into a brisk walk across what appeared as a pathless wilderness. The hoard's presence influenced the landscape around it. From out here the hoard appeared as a towering mountain peak, an island outpost amid a vast and trackless ocean if the ocean's water had petrified. The patterns of the topography even looked like waves frozen while rolling in toward a shore created by the hoard's solidity. Their group climbed up and down the swells, slipping on pebbles, clambering up steeper faces and half sliding down the slopes beyond. Negotiating the scalloped ground was rough going at first and got gentler as the hoard's influence faded and the rise and fall flattened out. The trunks of dead trees rose here and there, fragments of Realms that had fallen into the Beyond and died. The rib bones of forgotten giants carved arches against a backdrop of higher hills. Far away, a thin black line like an impossibly tall radio mast pierced into the silver sky, maybe a landmark, but, if so, not one she recognized.

Two hours passed at a steady tramp. If Shahin's feet hurt him in his dress shoes he said nothing. There was no wind, so no grit blew to smudge and streak his suit. Marianne was right about the suit. It was beautifully tailored and bizarrely out of place among a Hex crossing the Beyond in their practical gear.

Twice Gus directed them to avoid sumps that weren't visible to their eyes but which would have swallowed them were they to step within reach of hungry, sentient quicksand. Around them mist thickened and thinned at intervals. The hoard's peak would vanish as if behind fog and ten minutes later reappear.

No antic swarms disturbed them, for which Esther was grateful. She didn't know where Zosfadal's hoard was in relationship to the entrepôt they'd code-named Dunkirk. Thank goodness Daniel was already making friends and allies because there was no telling how long he would be stuck there. Had Chava answered her message? Would she do the sisterly thing and break her schedule to set up a guard on Kai, the babies, and the Keep?

The decision was out of her hands so there was no use wasting mental energy fretting over it. She fretted anyway.

Shahin nudged her and gestured to the horizon. Visible through the mist a pale city rose. Its towers and slender bridges were a marvel that beckoned as beauty always does. Irresistible and in this case deadly.

He murmured, "Shouldn't we check that out—"

Marianne hissed to cut him off.

Out ahead, Gus halted and turned in alarm. But he wasn't responding to Shahin's quiet question. He raised an open hand and closed it into a fist. The Hex looked over their shoulders. A light rose behind the island peak that marked the hoard, like sunrise.

Esther mouthed a curse. Bright was coming.

Marianne broke into a trot and barked, "Almost there. Move it."

The delicate city dissolved into swarms of antics. Maybe Shahin's whisper or Marianne's command had roused them, or perhaps they responded to the rising light that would soon obliterate the wilderness.

"Run," said Esther to Shahin. "Don't stop for anything. Follow Mar."

"What about you?"

"Go!"

They surged forward at an uneven lope, Marianne in the lead, Lydia stomping heavy-footed in her combat boots, Shahin with his faded rucksack bouncing clumsily against his suit jacket because he favored one leg. Gus held position out ahead. Faye shifted back to fall into step beside Esther, staff in one hand, ready to spin.

The cityscape had vanished. A seething storm of antics swept toward them, but the light grew stronger like a rising wave, and that was far worse. They could fight the antics. They couldn't fight the Bright.

Esther felt the pull of years in her creaking knees. She kept in shape but she wasn't thirty anymore. She wasn't even fifty anymore, which had once seemed old and ten years later seemed unbelievably young.

"Here! Here!" Marianne shouted, heedless of the approaching swarms.

She stood beside a modest rock cairn Esther hadn't seen. The Gate's feet braced as her left arm strained against an invisible force she held open. Lydia ducked under her arm and vanished. Shahin hesitated long enough that Faye prodded him hard in the back with her staff. He stumbled forward, popping out of sight, and the young woman piled in after. Gus jogged up and bent double, elbows tucked in to get inside the invisible tear in the mist. Then there wasn't time as the first stinging antics rushed in on them, eager to eat their memories and their lives.

Esther lit, just a small burst. The light drove the antics back for a few seconds, but Lantern magic also reached out and grasped at the Bright. Light called to light, the deadliest cycle of the Beyond tearing toward them across the flat ground.

Esther grabbed Marianne bodily to pull her in behind her as a shocking flash of icy blue-white radiance kindled the Beyond and obliterated everything that had once seemed to have substance. The tear in the fabric slammed shut with a boom.

10

Marianne staggered, shaking off Esther's hand. "Let me sit down," she said raggedly as she collapsed forward, breathing hard.

What felt like a storm swept in on the other side of the veil, the oasis shuddering and shifting as if it were a tent pitched in a gale.

"Close only counts in horseshoes and hand grenades," remarked Lydia. Her face was red from running but she grinned as she wiped perspiration from her brow. Close escapes always got the heart pumping. No one joined a Hex if they weren't a bit of an adrenaline junkie.

They stood panting on a lake shore. Reeds and trees ringed the dark water. Beyond the band of vegetation, an outer curtain of enmeshed vines grew up an irregular wall, so densely grown together that they blocked all view except a gap far overhead that at first glance seemed like a circular chimney opening but which was actually a translucent eye socket staring onto a white smear of sky.

Shahin looked around with wonder and dread. "Where are we?"

"Inside a dragon skull. A world eater, if I don't miss my guess. That's what we call the really big ones," said Esther.

"There are dragons big enough to eat worlds?"

"It's kind of a joke. Dragons are the only Realm-born creatures the Bright can't consume. Their bones can't be altered by Bright cycles, as other Realm-born objects can be. Are being, right now, if they haven't found shelter." She gestured in a circle to indicate the rumbling and howl from outside.

"Oh!" he said in a tone of sudden understanding.

"Haven't you traveled in the Beyond?" Esther asked.

He set down his rucksack and gave a pained sigh but no answer.

"Hold on," said Marianne, straightening. "If you've never traveled in the Beyond, then how did you get to Zosfadal's hoard in the first place? The only way through the Beyond is to walk."

"Walking isn't the *only* way," replied Esther, not wholly certain why she was leaping to Shahin's defense. "There are dragon scales, like the one we used."

"Sure there are," Marianne drawled, "but how would someone who isn't in a hoard or adjacent to the dragon get a scale before they had a relationship with the dragon?"

"That is surely a question," remarked Shahin.

Lydia chuckled.

He smiled slightly, then winced as his weight shifted onto his right leg and he quickly altered his stance onto his left.

Esther studied him. He didn't look out of breath but he sure looked like the one leg was hurting. "Huh. Okay. We need to set up camp and rest. Shahin, I'll fill you in on some Beyond basics you need for the trip."

All else aside, Marianne was tough. Recovering quickly, she hustled over to a small clearing with a fresh smile. "Good news. Bellflowers and a waypost."

The clearing was surrounded by unearthly purple-leafed

trees whose bell-shaped, translucent flowers swelled with liquid. Half the clearing had been bricked over to create an
oval platform with a brick hearth at one end and a wood
scaffolding over all.

"Luxury accommodations!" proclaimed Lydia with a grin.

Faye tapped the butt of her spear on the ground. "Hex at
seven o'clock."

The lake was round enough to make it easy to plot the shore-
line as if they were standing at twelve o'clock. Sure enough,
almost hidden by the vegetation, a thread of smoke gave away
the presence of another group. A Shotgun—the individual
carried a wicked-looking pike—had emerged from a stand of
what looked like bamboo to deliberately gaze across the water at them. No friendly signal. No flag of truce. Just a stare.

Lydia nodded. "Faye and I will do the necessary."

"The other Hex looks a bit hostile," remarked Shahin, although he spoke so levelly that it was difficult to tell if his
words were a simple observation or an anxious declaration.

Esther said, "Our Voice will ask to speak to their Voice.
They have to oblige because the Concilium requires these
protocols. If Hexes don't observe them, they're banned from
the Beyond. Shotguns go along to stand in back and look
dangerous, just in case we've encountered a rogue Hex that
doesn't intend to follow the rules."

As Esther was speaking, Lydia stripped out of the housecoat while Faye dug a poncho our of her backpack and handed
it to Esther. They trotted off toward the other Hex.

Marianne had already gotten to work like the experienced
Beyond traveler she was. She showed Shahin how to pinch
off the ends of the most swollen bellflowers so as not to break
their full sacs of liquid. They hurriedly collected as many as
they could into her upturned hat. Meanwhile, Esther strung

up the ponchos Kai had so carefully packed and used them to create a tarp-like roof. Marianne handed her a bug mesh so high-end it had a chameleon property that caused it to alter color to blend in against the foliage.

"This mesh isn't from Earth," said Esther as she secured tarp and mesh over the scaffolding to create a frame-like big tent.

"I'm not telling you where I got it." Marianne ducked inside with hat in hand.

"I wasn't going to ask."

Marianne cocked her head, listening. "Rain's here."

Shahin sank down to sit on the edge of the platform, then brushed at his hair with a look of alarm as it started to rain. "How can there be rain? Is that sleet?"

He scooted under the shelter as Lydia and Faye ran up and ducked inside. Marianne tied down the edges of the bug mesh to seal them in. Gus gave them a wave from outside. Still intangible inside an oasis, he would stay out on patrol.

"You make contact?" Esther asked.

"Yes, briefly." Lydia roughly brushed off several bugs crawling up a sleeve and stomped on them. "Their Voice was hard to understand. They didn't use any of the formal courtesy phrases we learn. They didn't say where they're from. If I had to guess, I'd wonder if they're from a recently opened Realm. Maybe a Schedule Three about to move up to Schedule Four. I'm guessing they're a self-formed Hex local to their Realm scoping out this unknown situation they've discovered."

Like Daniel's father's family, fifty years ago, Esther thought.

Faye said, "Freelancers like us?"

Lydia nodded. "No clan or enterprise banner. No Concilium-issued badges. If they are rogue freelancers, it explains why they are suspicious of us."

"Huh." Esther peered through the trees toward the other side of the lake. The rain had really started coming down, turning the view into a shimmering curtain of water. "I wonder if I should put them into contact with Chava's associates."

"Now is not the time to go trying to make friends with a trigger-happy novice Hex with no reason to trust us," said Marianne. "We've been down this road before, Esther. Literally this road, which clearly I'm the only one willing to remind you led from one thing to another and eventually to the five triangles gambit, which as we all know literally led to our suspension. Which has fucked me over big-time, for one. I know the rest of you think it's all about the money for me, but that wasn't the issue. The issue is that I could have made different arrangements financially if I'd known in advance instead of being blindsided because Esther decided she could dictatorially make a decision which affected all of us so materially. For all you know, I would have gone along with the plan, if I'd only been given the courtesy of being consulted instead of manipulated. You overstepped, Esther. You didn't trust me, or the others. I can't speak for the rest of the Hex, and since no one has talked to me in a year, I'm just a bit confused as to why they're all still so cozy with you."

Esther sat quietly under this tirade. Marianne had the right to be angry. When she was sure the other woman had no more to say, she answered. "That's a fair criticism. Anyway, right now I'm not launching any tangents. Not until Daniel is home."

Shahin had been watching the exchange with startled interest.

Lydia swept her right arm in an orator's gesture. "I'd like to finish my report without further interruption. I told the

82

other Hex we had our own business and weren't interested in theirs. If they're novices, they won't be a match for us in a fight. There's no benefit to them starting one inside an oasis anyway. Just a feeling I have, but folks like this rarely survive the Beyond, especially if this is their first crossing."

"I wouldn't be so sure," retorted Marianne. "They knew how to get into this oasis. Sussing out the presence of an oasis is not elementary Gate magic, not like cutting an opening in or out of a Keep. So either they figured it out on their own, or they got basic training. And our Faye is pretty new herself so I'm surprised you aren't worried about her being up to taking Trey's place. He never backed down from any threat. You shouldn't haven't accepted his retirement. We'd be better off."

Esther shook her head. "Really, Mar? You're going after Faye now?"

"I think she's still going after you, Esther. I don't take it personally." Faye had an enigmatic smile and, like all the best Shotguns, a calm focus that was difficult to upset.

"Faye is our storm wind astride a lion," declaimed Lydia. "Shall I sing her praises?"

"Please, don't," said Marianne. "If I have to hear another story about your triumph at the theater of Pergamon in front of ten thousand cheering fans and the king too, I'll throw you out into the Bright."

"You'll try," said Lydia.

"Truce," said Esther. This was why they hadn't met as a group since the suspension but she knew better than to say so out loud. "Let's eat."

Stretched taut, the ponchos withstood the steady rain that showed no sign of letting up. The wind thrummed outside. The temperature dropped even further. Drops of water clinging to branches froze into ice. Lydia got a fire going and they sat around its warmth as they ate the delicious rugelach and savory rolls as well as sharing a wedge of waybread. By pinching the tip of the closed bellflowers they could drink the liquid inside. The sweet sap like ginger syrup refreshed the palate.

Faye said, "What did you decide to do this past year, Lydia? I tried to contact you a couple of times. I even sent an actual letter to the postbox address Esther gave me."

"Oh dear. My apologies, young storm wind. I never checked it. I joined a touring company. The grind keeps me out of trouble. You look good."

"I did a lot of physical therapy. I wanted to be ready. I feel ready."

"You are, my young padawan." They both laughed as Lydia made *pew-pew* noises. Shahin scratched his head, looking adorably puzzled.

Marianne ignored the others as she paged through her personal chartbook of the Beyond, making notations like the responsible Gate she was. She was an excellent Gate but with every passing year in the Hex she'd clashed more and more with the others. Sometimes Hex dynamics fell out that way, as had happened with Trey when he'd started drinking too much, and in fact Marianne had been the one who had pushed him hardest to retire, even if she conveniently glossed over that now.

"You should eat." Esther offered a pastry, a roll, and waybread to Shahin. He raised a hand to refuse it. "I'm offering freely, no charge, no obligation."

"Why would you do that?" he asked.

"Why? Because I'm a decent person, and decent people share because it makes the world a better place."

Marianne snorted.

Esther added, "I can see why someone under the claw of a boss might not trust the idea of decency. If that isn't a persuasive argument for you, then I offer a self-interested option. A Hex needs to stay strong. If you get weak from hunger or thirst it puts us all in danger."

He thought this over and accepted the waybread but not, she noticed, either of the items that had been baked in the hoard's kitchen.

After he'd eaten, he asked, "Will it stop raining soon?"

"It won't stop raining here inside the oasis until the Bright passes. I wouldn't leave the platform."

She indicated the mesh, where gnats and triple-winged centipedes were colliding with the screen, scenting the presence of Realm-born creatures. Bugs were emerging from the ground, roused by the life-giving rain of the Bright. A pile of boncs lay half buried beneath the trunk of a bellflower tree, whose buds swelled as the rain engorged them.

"I see what you mean. Is there a place I can change my clothing?"

"We will all politely turn our backs."

"Sure we will," said Marianne in the same tone she'd used to call Kai a pretty fish. When everyone gave her a pointed stare, she put away her chartbook and, grumbling under her breath, hung up a privacy screen for the portable toilet that could double as a dressing room.

When he went behind the screen to change, Esther called the others into a huddle. Their heads bent together, she whispered.

"The boss is demanding to trade Daniel for Kai. That's why we are headed to Dunkirk. Zosfadal was cagey about what he told me. What I do know is he made some kind of trade that Kai figured in—"

"Five years ago, you mean," said Marianne.

"That's what I figure. It would fit the timeline. He got the goods but he didn't deliver Kai."

"Are you saying the delivery didn't go through because the entrepôt collapsed?" Faye asked. "Isn't that what happened?"

"It's complicated, but that's how I see it, yes. What matters to Zosfadal is that the debt has come back to him. We're going to Dunkirk to see if we can find out who he was trading with. Maybe I can negotiate a deal directly with whoever that is. I also suspect there is something else going on."

"Can you perhaps be more specific?" Lydia murmured sardonically.

Esther glanced toward the screen and hoped they were far enough away that Shahin couldn't overhear. "Kai has been adamant about not trying to contact kwos birth clan."

"Kwo?" Marianne interrupted. "I thought Kai used male pronouns."

"On Earth and around Daniel he generally does. But Kai has explained that within dragon kindreds the correct term is kwo. And before you ask, that's all I know. May I go on?"

Marianne got a calculating look in her eyes. "I'd give a lot to know more about dragon kindreds and how they function. I feel like they give Hexes a few magic tricks, the ones we have to get us through the Beyond and make us useful to them. But the really valuable magic, like shape-shifting, they withhold from us humanoids."

"If that ability is even magic," said Lydia. "Maybe it's just an adaptive part of their physiology."

"Like yours?" asked Marianne sharply.

Lydia smiled enigmatically. "I am a curious case, it's true. There's a lot I don't even know about myself, but I stay more or less human, don't I? My point is, we know nothing about the Realm the dragons come from, much less what other life forms look like there and what that might tell us about them."

Esther nodded. "Wouldn't we all like to know more. Anyway, Kai once told me the Joseph story made kwo think of home. That makes me wonder if it was Kai's own family who sold kwo to slavers. How Zosfadal's Hex got hold of Kai is unknown. Also, the boss refused to reveal the identity of the enterprise he was trading with in Dunkirk. He *also* wouldn't say what he got in return that he can't give back to resolve the debt."

Faye raised her right hand like a tentative student. "There is one thing I've always wondered. Isn't cross-species reproduction impossible? I mean, Kai is what *we* call a dragon. But on Earth, Kai has to pass as human except in the family. I get that some dragons can shape-shift to travel incognito in Realms. But how can Kai and Daniel have had children together? That's what I'm not clear on. Most Earth folks just take the relationship in stride, like most people do these days. Those who have questions seem to assume either that Kai is a trans man, if they saw Kai pregnant, or think they are two gay men who arranged for an assisted reproduction surrogate. Which conveniently explains the quadruplets. But I've never heard a single person in the *family* talk about, like, literally biologically how it could happen."

"Those babies are awfully cute even with the third eye," admitted Marianne with a rare genuine smile. "Little rascals, too. Last time I saw them they couldn't have been much more than a year old and climbing anything, I swear. Way too agile for humans."

Esther nodded. "Like Mar said, basically we know almost nothing about dragons because they don't want us to know anything about them, especially not anything as crucial and personal as reproduction." She signed for silence as the screen's fabric swayed, Shahin moving around behind it. "Let's table this discussion for later. Rest while we have the chance."

Lydia took first watch. Esther unrolled her sleeping pad and sleep sack alongside Faye and Marianne. She fell asleep quickly, a skill acquired during her stint in the navy decades ago.

A moment later Faye gently shook her awake.

"Six hours?" Esther asked softly.

"All quiet," she said before turning in.

Esther peed, poured powder on the urine to solidify it for disposal in the Beyond, and sanitized her hands. The rain fell as steadily as before, and the air was a little warmer. The early watch had allowed the fire to burn down to embers while they were all tucked snug into warm sacks. She unzipped her sleep sack and wrapped it around her as a cloak, then sat cross-legged on the sleeping pad to watch the lake. The sleet had warmed back into a rain pounding on the water. Fish jumped to feast on the banquet of bugs. Their strange shapes and stranger colors dazzled her, neither stranger nor more mundane than Earth-based water life.

She savored a second rugelach, the crisp bite of the exterior, the flaky, buttery layers, the sweet filling of chopped nuts. Daniel had shown an aptitude for cooking and baking early on, making a mess in the kitchen, obsessed with cooking shows. Both his bubbe and his tutu had shared unwritten recipes with him before they passed. How was he doing? Was he still in the kitchen? Had he been forced back into the cage?

Esther hated this feeling of helplessness, of knowing that even the best she did might not be enough. She did gamble too much with reckless actions that would either succeed modestly or fail spectacularly. Marianne wasn't wrong about that. But sometimes gambling was all a person had when the monstrous guns were a-roar and the only path lay forward into the fire.

Gus ghosted into view and gave her a thumbs-up. The other Hex's Ghost walked alongside him. Detente? They both seemed relaxed as they headed on around the lake shore, not that either could cause harm to the other.

Shahin sat down cross-legged next to her. He tucked up a calf-length robe to reveal loose trousers beneath. A front-opening riding coat, something like a kaftan, covered the whole. He rested a brimmed cap on one knee. Except for the sunglasses, he might have walked out of a fifteenth-century miniature painting depicting a scene from the *Shah-Nameh*. The sunglasses remained, and the funniest part was that they genuinely looked great with the ensemble. It was almost too much but because it wasn't quite, that just made him even more distinctive.

Whoa, Esther. It had been ten years since Vincent's death, and she'd kept busy because she liked busy and also because she had a lot to do and also because it kept her from dwelling too much on how she'd set aside the idea of opening up her life to another partner someday, tomorrow, never. He was a boss's lieutenant, for goodness' sakes. Not a potential hookup for a giddy twenty-year-old.

"I understand the disembodied one acts as a scout," he said, gesturing toward the trees. "But the rain and the bugs inside here do not touch him."

Thank goodness Shahin had no clue what she was thinking. She was grateful for a chance to explain, anything to move her careening thoughts to a neutral subject. "That's the benefit of intangibility for scouting. The downside is he can't speak to us, even inside an oasis. That's why we use sign language."

"The Ghost does not eat or sleep with the rest of you."

"That's right. Ghosts don't need to eat, drink, or sleep when in the Beyond."

"He carries a pack."

"Yes, because Hexes travel into Realms. He carries his own gear and also things our Hex will only need in Realms. Is this really your first time in the Beyond?" He seemed about to speak, but did not. "Do you need me to give a quick rundown of the necessary rules of traveling in the Beyond?"

"I would not say no."

She smiled. "I'll accept that as a yes. I'm afraid I really love to give speeches. I have a background in communications. My apologies in advance. Are you a poet?"

The sunglasses turned on her, blank and depthless. "The rules for travel in the Beyond."

"I won't ask again." She offered him the last rugelach, which he again refused, so she set it aside for Marianne, who wouldn't have taken a watch shift yet. "I don't know how much time we'll have so I'll keep it simple. There are three rules that matter most for survival. First of all, never travel during the Bright, only during the Pitch or the Gloam. A Gloam is what separates Pitch and Bright. The Bright will disintegrate you. Second, when traveling through the Beyond don't speak except in an emergency. Speech attracts antics and other creatures. They seek consciousness. That city we saw, for example. Swarms must have devoured the consciousness of people who lived in such a place in a Realm. When they settled to rest, they settled themselves into a model of the city that lived in the memories they consumed."

"How terrible."

"For those whose minds they devoured, yes. Third, leave nothing behind in an oasis like this one because it upsets the delicate ecological balance that maintains the oasis itself."

"What about the bones under that bush? Those were left behind."

"One lost traveler can be absorbed. Twenty would strain the system and begin to poison the oasis, turn it into a sludge of toxic algae, or rafts of decomposing fungus, or worse. Then we Hexes would lose havens that allow us to cross the Beyond."

"I understand the six-sided magic of a Hex. But I'm not quite clear on where their authority or permission to travel comes from. All the Hexes I have encountered at the hoard have had some kind of official badge."

"The Concilium runs all oversight on the Beyond. Well, all the oversight they can. Even dragons can't see and know everything, thank goodness. Zosfadal is miserly when it comes to sharing information with you. Typical hoarder."

His lips twitched.

"Caught you," she said, and this time he did smile. She grinned, feeling stupidly proud of herself. *Move on, move on, Esther. This is not the time.* "The main thing is, the Concilium certifies official Hexes and allows them to function under Concilium oversight."

"Your Hex was suspended."

"That's right. Because we are freelancers we didn't have a dragon clan or an approved enterprise to defend us at the Concilium. It was easy to make an example of us for what a clan-supported Hex might have gotten away with. Earth is a minor trading post, a Schedule Four Realm. Most of our population doesn't know the Beyond exists. We humans that do know are struggling to stake a claim to autonomy for Earth. In other words, we're not at all important in the greater scheme of things from the point of view of the Concilium. No one even knows how long outsiders have been running operations on Earth without our knowledge. Decades? Centuries?"

"What your son called 'an exploited Realm.'"

"Not unlike Earth's own history. But that's a different conversation and not really germane to our immediate issue of survival while traveling in the Beyond."

"The point you're making is that Hexes are the main means of non-dragon movement. According to what I have observed, no group larger than six ever attempts to travel together in the Beyond."

"That's right. Hexes can camp or move in proximity to each other as long as they are not too close in any configuration greater than six individuals. Too much Realm destabilizes the Beyond. Often quite spectacularly, and with fatal results. A very long time ago, so the story goes, an autocrat didn't believe what he'd been told and tried to march an army through the Beyond to wage war on an enemy."

"Like Kabujiya's army in the desert of Mudreya."

"Mudreya?"

"You might also say . . . Misr?"

"Egypt! Do you mean Cambyses, Cyrus's son? You know Earth history?"

He looked away from her, even though the sunglasses already hid his eyes. "More than six is too many, then. But a Hex often travels as five, since Keepers rarely travel. I wonder if one person can travel in the Beyond."

"Alone?" She huffed a laugh. "Sure, anyone can travel if

they can get into the Beyond. The question is getting out of it. Each member of a Hex provides a useful skill for survival."

"Because the Ghost scouts. The Shamshir fights. The Gate opens and closes."

"That's right. Gates can open gates between the Beyond and the Realms, and in the Beyond a Gate follows landmarks. They're pathfinders. That's how we travel without getting lost. I'm a Lantern. I make light when needed. Most creatures of the Beyond are light-averse because the Bright is so deadly. I can also create a kind of mirror shield in an emergency. My senses are pretty acute as well, and I have good night vision. Other than that I'm useless so I try to be up-to-date about all the Concilium codes and contractual fine print."

"Knowledge is a form of light," he said.

"It is, isn't it? Huh. That's very kind of you to say so." She smiled at him.

He did not smile back, so she shifted uncomfortably and went on. "The Voice speaks. You heard Lydia describe her parlay with the Voice of the other Hex. Sentient and humanoid beings enter the Beyond from multiple Realms. They have to be able to talk to each other. Keepers are our anchors. Lighthouses. Beacons. Hmm. I'm not sure how to explain it."

"A Keeper is also a Voice."

"No. Oh! You're wondering how everyone could speak to Daniel in the hoard."

"Yes."

"Because so many groups may move in and out of a Keep, a Keeper also acts as a kind of universal translator. Every language-using creature within a set distance from a Keeper will be able to speak in an intelligible way to the Keeper. Daniel's really good with dogs, too. And he can calm people down or even put them to sleep. It's a protective spell all Keepers need in case of trouble in their Keep, so while he may seem like a pushover, a cupcake, if you will, he's not." She glanced at him as her curiosity flared. "You and I are still speaking in what sounds to me as English. The Keeper-effect should have worn off when we left the hoard."

"I know English," he said.

"How on Earth do you know English?"

"It was a requirement for the job."

"The job of Zosfadal's lieutenant?"

He shrugged, which she was coming to see was his way of putting off an answer he didn't want to or couldn't give.

"It is odd your boss knew what the term 'Wild West' meant. Huh."

He adjusted his sunglasses but did not remove them. "You say 'huh' when you've had a thought."

"Yes, it annoys my children to no end." She grinned. "Anyway, the last piece of a Hex is that a Hex can bring a sixth person in the Keeper's place, since the Keeper stays in the Keep. Six is advantageous in the Beyond. More stable than other configurations for reasons we don't know. A lot of this isn't information the dragons share but what we've put together on our own. This sixth person is often called Cargo, although that's a bit discourteous."

"So I am Cargo." His smile was unexpected and appealingly wry.

"Just be happy you're not a slave or prisoner. You noticed the incoming Hex when we left the hoard. Their Cargo looked abused to me, sweating, exhausted, carrying a heavy object bigger than their own body. Disgraceful."

"You do have strong opinions, Star of Evening."

"I do. Very strong opinions. The badge that Hex was wearing matched the pattern on your tie. Zosfadal runs his own Hex, doesn't he?"

She didn't expect Shahin to answer, and he did not, but he didn't get up and leave either.

After a moment, she went on. "Any questions so far?"

"A hoard I understand. I have now visited an oasis. A Keep allows access to a Realm. I have heard it is also true an extension of a Realm can exist in the Beyond."

"Yes, those are what we call entrepôts and peninsulas. Other languages and peoples have different terms for them. They're like hoards in being physically solid but unlike hoards in that it isn't a dragon's magic that creates them. They aren't restricted to dragons, I mean. Any humanoid Realm can create its own peninsula with six closely sited Keeps. An entrepôt is created at the convergence of the Keeps of six different Realms instead of just one."

"A trade city where many routes meet," he said as his eyes narrowed. He was thinking hard, and not sharing one bit of that thinking with her. Was he a secretive man or simply unable to talk because of his relationship to Zosfadal? Hard to say.

They sat in silence as the rain fell. When he said nothing more, she fished out her field notebook and wrote down shorthand observations about Zosfadal's hoard together with an account of her conversation with the boss, in case she needed to remember it precisely later.

As she finished, she looked up to see he was staring at the lake with a pensive expression on his striking face. In some ways, mystery could make a person attractive. But it might also be a big red *Danger!* flag.

Sensing her gaze, he glanced over at her and smiled as if in apology. Oh dear. His contrite smile was horribly charming.

"I have not yet thanked you for your generous sharing of information," he said. "I do that now. My thanks."

"You're welcome. In fairness, although I do aspire to be generous, filling you in is as important to the Hex's safety as to yours." She hadn't given up seeing if she could learn anything more about Zosfadal, his hoard, or Shahin for that matter. It was worth a try. "Basically, this talk boils down to two things. Stay close to us, and follow our directions."

"But people do travel in the Beyond who aren't Hexes."

Interesting. This was the first time he had circled back to a subject.

"You mean like those 'applicants' waiting at the entrance to the hoard." She thought of the singers who had surged to Daniel's Keep. Had they made it to the top of the tower? Were they still alive up there, hoping the Keep would open soon? If—*when*—Daniel returned, what would they do? What did they want? "More survive in the Beyond than folk might think. They could be condemned prisoners dumped into the Beyond to die. They could be refugees desperate enough to take the risk. Reckless thrill-seekers who may not have figured out what a bad choice they made until it's too late and they can't return to where they came from. But no Realm-born creature can survive indefinitely in the Beyond. By the time people reach a dragon's hoard, or an entrepôt or a peninsula or a Keep, they're likely desperate enough to take whatever terms they're offered, even if it amounts to indentured servitude. What is the population of Zosfadal's hoard these days?"

Shahin smiled cryptically.

"I had to try," she said. "I should add that entrepôts

aren't necessarily exploitative places. Most are ordinary cross-Realm market towns where people enjoy a mix of cultures and the hustle of life. It's just they can't safely go sightseeing outside the town gates. A few Schedule Six Realms even have refugee programs, although as with everything you have to do your research so you don't find yourself slaving in a salt mine."

"I can't tell if that is a figure of speech or if there are actual slaves in salt mines."

She rubbed at her lower lip with a finger. "Seeing the Hex and the bustle of the warehouse makes me think about how much trade must be going in and out of Zosfadal's hoard. Everything that was in that kitchen, like salt. All those books and scrolls. And the caged person. Not to mention the metal beast and the chimera."

Shahin's hands, clasped loosely on his lap, tightened. "You are assuming the chimera was traded in."

"How else could a chimera get there? But they are meant to be mythological creatures anyway, so am I seeing it as a chimera when really it is something else? I do that all the time."

"I'm not sure I follow."

"Some of the people on Earth who know about the Beyond believe that many of the fantastical creatures described in Earth's stories and myths might represent sightings of beings that came from other Realms. I've never seen any evidence of that. Not that I know for sure, mind you. The thing is, I describe people and beings and objects with terms that are familiar to me. All that means is that Earth is my frame of reference, not that those things are what I call them. Which still doesn't explain where the chimera came from, does it? Because I saw it with my own eyes."

He said softly, "You are assuming its physical being came from a Realm rather than originating in the hoard itself."

"What does that mean?"

"'There are more things on heaven and earth than are dreamt of in your philosophy.'"

"Shakespeare?"

He shrugged evasively, clearly not intending to explain himself. Again.

"That quote was a distraction," she said accusingly.

As if a heavenly spigot had been turned off, the rain stopped. A warming breeze rustled branches. Water dripped from leaves. A splash in the lake was followed by silence as all the humming bugs sank into slumber.

The itch of her unanswered question must go unscratched. It wasn't even as if he'd beaten her in a game of who could say less, but that she'd understood all along he was holding back. Setting aside the sting of curiosity and a flicker of pointless annoyance, she got to her feet and brushed off her hands.

"Bright's over. Time to move."

11

Esther woke the others. With the ease of practice they dismantled their camp, ran a final check over the ground to make sure they'd left nothing behind, and assembled beside Marianne at the edge of the oasis. Marianne cut a tear into the vines. Gus ducked through and, sixteen seconds later, returned to fetch her.

They were gone a full three minutes. During that time the members of the other Hex moved up through the trees along the shore. Was there going to be trouble? Faye shifted to place herself in fighting position. Lydia greeted them, but they kept their distance and their Voice did not reply. They were watching, not precisely hostile. Waiting, but for what? It was hard to tell because their faces were obscured by dark scarves wrapped around their heads, as if they were cold or perhaps wanted to hide their faces.

Marianne squeezed through the opening. "Good news. The Bright uncovered the spine connected to this skull. That gives us a ridgeway to follow. I hope you're up for an eight- or ten-hour hike. Based on the landmarks I'm seeing, there's a good chance the spine will bring us within an hour of Damascus. Then we just have to get into and through to Twin Keep without being arrested, after which it's an easy walk across the Keep's concourse to the entry to Dunkirk. I'm *sure* Esther can manage the border agents like she manages everything else."

"A fortunate Bright," remarked Lydia, ignoring Marianne's sarcastic finish.

"Damascus," Shahin said.

"Our name for a specific entrepôt," said Esther. "We learn the local names but we use our own English shorthand while traveling as a form of verbal map. D names link close to D names. M names close to M. You get the picture. We also try to give them names that reflect something about our experience of them. In the ancient and medieval world Damascus was a significant and prosperous multicultural crossroads."

"Dimašq," he murmured.

Lydia shot him a curious look and said something in what Esther was pretty sure was Arabic, to which he replied briefly. Esther would have asked, but there wasn't time and he wouldn't have answered anyway.

Marianne caught sight of the other Hex standing about thirty yards away. "Let's get out of here. What if they aren't experienced enough to understand they can't get too close?"

They left the safety of the oasis. In this cycle of Gloam there was no mist, just a background haze. It smelled of sulfur, making Esther's nostrils sting until she fished out a mask and hooked it over her face to filter the fumes. The others weren't as sensitive, but her sinuses were already threatening to riot.

From the outside the oasis could only be seen if the observer realized they were seeing a reflection of the surrounding landscape. An oasis was a strange phenomenon, a stable zone with a footprint both in the Beyond and in the solidity of a Realm, although you couldn't pass through it into a connected Realm without a Keep. Most people would walk right past without knowing the oasis was there. Even knowing she had just emerged through a barrier, it was difficult for her to recognize the haven waiting close by.

The dragon's spine was something else entirely. It appeared as a bone-white ridge that stretched into the hazy distance with no sign of an end. The Hex scrambled to the top and caught their breath. Shahin turned a full circle, staring open-mouthed. Faye did a goofy little dance of excitement, nothing noisy or outrageous. It was her first dragon spine. Even Marianne smiled along with the rest at the Shotgun's glee.

Esther scanned the surroundings. Instead of the grit-streaked rolling surface they'd hiked across to get here, the landscape had been scoured flat by the just-passed Bright. The desolate scene stretched to what passed for a horizon. Sparks embedded in the dark ground winked on and off. Zosfadal's peak had vanished but the mysterious spire was still visible.

Shahin opened his mouth, then remembered Esther's warning and choked back the words. Marianne led the way along the ridgetop. Their footfalls kicked up a chalklike dust that reminded Esther of the crushed and polished detritus of seashells.

When Faye nudged her, Esther looked back to see the other Hex trailing about one hundred yards behind. Had the Hex always planned to come this way, or were they following them? The scarves concealed every part of their head except a slit for eyes. They appeared to have two arms and two legs and had a gait so humanlike that Esther wondered if they were human or close cousins. A sibling species? The Realms had been connected through the Beyond for a span of time known only to dragons, who according to lore were the first to travel between. Dragons also claimed they were the only beings capable of fastening a Realm to the Beyond by means of a word that roughly meant "stake" or "post." According to legend, the original Keepers had all been dragons. Some even whispered that humanoids who became Keepers among the many other sapient species had a trace of dragon ancestry. Esther had long scoffed at the notion. How could such hybrids happen? Now she was grandmother to four toddler hybrids.

Another theory suggested the six members of a Hex were humanoid reflections of the magic wielded by the six dragon kindreds. Stone was a Keeper, who sat stable atop earth. Water was a Voice, fluid and able to move into any branching stream. Metal was a Gate who could cut. Fire was a weapon that could both protect and destroy. Air was a Lantern, since her light had no heat, merely brightness. Aether was Ghost, intangible, pure, and immutable.

It was as good a theory as any.

Since dragons hoarded knowledge as well as anything else they could cover with their wings and grip with their claws, they weren't about to share any more secrets or history, or technology, philosophy, biology, or even basic tips than they had to in order to allow Hex traffic to get them what they wanted when they wanted it. She was pretty sure they weren't "dragons" in the Earth sense either, but rather that they appeared in a form meant to instill awe and fear. Form was also part of language. If any one thing stitched together the many Realms and made it possible for interaction to go on, it was communication in its varied forms.

This random woolgathering helped to keep thoughts of Daniel at bay as they hiked onward. He'd be cooking and chatting. Kai would be worrying. The babies could be a handful, chock-full of energy and giggles and mischief. Well, there was family just up the lane in the big compound. Kai wouldn't be alone. Still, she hoped Chava would heed the summons.

Every hour they halted for a few minutes to rest their feet, drink a little, and eat a sliver of the nourishing waybread. Lydia would usually perform a brief mime to entertain them. Sometimes they played a round of silent charades, which Gus always won because he was the most adept at signing the answer quickly, which invariably annoyed the hyper-competitive Marianne. The hardest part of a Beyond journey was staying relaxed but alert. Their long-established routines served them well. Shahin still wore his dress shoes, and he still limped, but she'd forgotten to ask, and he probably wouldn't have answered, and it wouldn't have mattered regardless because he kept up.

Behind them, the unknown Hex halted when they halted and walked when they walked, coming no closer, falling no farther behind.

The twilight and the flat land remained quiet and still.

After seven hours, unnervingly quiet and still.

Esther expected the Gloam to fade toward Pitch but it stayed as it was, the same haze, the same endless flat like a dry salt lake bed stretching into infinity, hairline cracks marking intriguing patterns like all the questions she had that kept splitting into more questions.

When they halted at the seven-hour mark Lydia didn't bother with entertainment. Everyone was checking their watches, looking for an end to the spine that seemed to stretch on into infinity. A prickling sense of perilous expectation made her want to jump back up and start jogging. By

Marianne's nervous glance skyward and Gus's restless pacing, they felt it too. Lydia scanned the flats. Faye kept her gaze on the trailing Hex. Shahin sat with head bowed, eyes invisible behind his sunglasses.

"Shit." Marianne clambered to her feet. It was shocking to hear a human voice. She shaded her eyes as she stared back the way they'd come. "Double Bright. Bonfire coming. We have to take cover."

They all turned to look and, in turning, caused the trailing Hex to look over their shoulders. The dim haze behind them lightened with a golden-red color at the farthest line of sight, an unseen fireball rolling toward them as it gathered size and momentum. Out on the flats, sparks embedded in the ground began winking more frequently. Buried antics might stir in this way, digging free. Other creatures might slither through the ground or spew parts of themselves to coat any wanderers in a slime that would absorb their living energy.

Esther got to her feet, knees twinging, a warning pain in her ankle as she bent it awkwardly in her haste. "Lydia, with me."

She started toward the other Hex.

"Are you crazy?" Marianne demanded to her back.

Lydia hurried up beside Esther. "Are you?"

"If they're inexperienced, we have to warn them. We'd be responsible if they died when we might have prevented it."

The other Hex stood. Their Voice and their Ghost came forward to meet equidistant between the two groups. Seen through a narrow gap in the head wrap, the Ghost's eyes seemed strangely human, although that was unlikely.

Lydia spoke words Esther could not understand, in a tone infused with urgency. Their Voice struggled to answer, as if they had poor command of the language, and Lydia repeated herself patiently. After thirty agonizing seconds of confusion, a third person came forward and with rough gestures identified themselves as the Lantern of the Hex.

Esther addressed Lydia as she gestured to include the Lantern. "Tell them that to survive what is coming, their Lantern must create a dome of light and then reverse it and keep it reversed until the Bonfire has passed. It reflects the light to create a shield against the Bright. Do they know how to do this?"

An unintelligible exchange rapidly passed between the members of the unknown Hex.

"Now!" cried Esther.

Their Lantern spoke. Their Voice spoke.

Lydia said, "They know the procedure. They add thanks for the gracious warning."

"No worries. Let's go."

Lydia barked a final comment, more command than farewell. They ran back to their own. Heat gusted past in rising waves. The saltlike grains of the flats began to steam and then to boil, releasing clouds of antics and worse things but there was no time to register what or how swiftly these threats were moving toward the dragon's spine. A fiery light flared hot and brilliant as if it were the coronal mass ejection of a sun. In thirty seconds more its forward tip would reach them and obliterate their fragile bodies.

Esther dropped to the ground, positioning herself at the middle of the spine's flat ridgetop. The others sat around her, even disembodied Gus.

She lit. Her light created a completely sealed chamber, a circular floor beneath and a dome above, pulled tight until it just covered them. A desperate swarm of antics battered against the light, a few squeezing through as if past finest mesh.

In her mind she framed the dome of light as prosaically as if it were a sock, and she reversed it, flipping it inside out. The outside flashed white.

All view of the outside vanished as the reversal took effect. They sheltered in a dome of sealed darkness whose light projected outward.

Mar yelped as an antic stung her. Faye flipped out one of her fans and there followed a series of slaps and swishes. A final tiny buzz, a last whap, and merciful silence.

"Got them all," said Faye.

"Why on Earth did a nice, well-educated young woman like you get into a trash gig like this?" Marianne demanded.

Esther swore she could hear Faye's sly grin. "This is still less stressful than working in publishing."

The wind hit, or maybe it was molten waves, jolting them as if they were a coracle caught in a tempest at sea, thrown hither and yon, sliding, tossed. They grasped hold of each other, trying to position the backpacks to catch the worst of the battering each time the chamber spun all the way around or tipped hard to one side, once almost perpendicular before righting itself. A thunderous roar hammered at them, so loud they could not be heard even if they shouted.

Had they been flung off the spine? Impossible to know.

Reversing her light was an emergency measure. It blocked their sight and Gus's senses, and Marianne couldn't cut through it. They might end up anywhere, flung to a region even the Gate did not know from her extensive study of landmarks of the Beyond, all the best real estate, Esther thought wildly as the dome spun all the way around as in a tornado. Her shoulder slammed against a hard surface, pain throbbing, but she had to hold on to the light. If the reversed chamber dissolved they would be burned to nothing, not even ash left. Her ears throbbed. Her hands ached with heat, knuckles on fire. Her throat parched and her entire body hurt. But she knew how to hold on as life assaulted her. Death, loss, reversals, these plunges into a pit out of which a person had to climb as against a stiff wind or a sharp wall or else lie in the ditch until the flooding waters drowned you.

She breathed out through barely parted lips to ease the old creak of healed ribs and the spot where she'd once been kicked in the hip that ached when stressed.

Silence came with a bump. A smooth slide to an easy stop. Stillness.

12

The heat dissipated. The worst had passed.

Esther tried to speak but her mouth was too dry.

Lydia said, "Count off."

"I think I broke my shoulder," said Marianne.

"Do you mean that?" Lydia asked sharply.

"I hope not. Fuck."

"I'm fine," said Faye, although the tightness in her voice suggested she was shaken up.

Gus said nothing but he would be unaffected by the wild ride.

Shahin said, hoarsely, "What was that?"

"Bonfire Bright," said Marianne as she rubbed her shoulder. "Evil twin to Icy Bright. Since Icy Bright is already evil you can see how bad it would have been to be caught out in it."

Shahin murmured, "'Some say the world will end in fire, some say in ice.'"

Esther managed to moisten her mouth enough to speak. "Did you major in Earth literature?"

"What does 'major' mean in this context? A thing of significance? A military rank?"

"Never mind. I'm surprised you know so much Earth-based poetry."

He recited something in Chinese.

Lydia laughed, and replied in that language, then said, "Of course I prefer Li Bai, but I like my wine."

"You studied Earth literature in multiple languages. Right." Esther sighed. "Never mind. Mar? How is your shoulder really? Do we need to splint it?"

Beside her, bumping up against her because space was so tight, Marianne manipulated and moved her arm. "I guess it's only bruised but wow does it hurt. The good news is we are still on the spine. It should be safe to open up."

"'Should be,'" muttered Shahin.

"That's the spirit!" said Esther with a laugh made harsh by her dry throat.

She groped for her hip flask and held it out. The others took a sip and handed it back to her for her own swig. The pure burn gave her the energy she needed to douse the light. The dome vanished as if swallowed with the whiskey, a shield one instant and then gone as if it had never existed.

They were still seated on the dragon's spine but had been blown all the way to its tail end, mere steps from a steep, short drop to the ground. The landscape had changed utterly. Multiple crevices cut the once-flat plain, making the ground impassable where it had split apart, every crack now a chasm. There was no sign of the other Hex on the spine and certainly not anywhere on the riven ground.

Esther rubbed her eyes, so bone weary that she couldn't imagine how to stand. Had the other Hex died even though they'd tried to warn them? Had the Beyond devoured them? At times like this she half believed the Beyond had consciousness, as if the physical aspects of the Beyond were a corpus, as if an intangible mind poured a Bright through itself hoping to catch and absorb the minds and energy of interlopers crawling unwanted and unasked across its magical flesh. The Beyond was minding its own business, wasn't it? It hadn't asked to become a pathway for all these traveling creatures. Maybe it was fighting back in the only way it could, or maybe she should have tried harder to make sure the other Hex had understood her warning.

No. This was dangerous mental wandering, to which she was prone when exhausted. She'd done her best, even if it never seemed to be enough. Even if you would never know the outcome of the work you did, you had to keep doing the work.

Faye stared toward the entrepôt, hands outstretched as if warming cold fingers at a fire of astonishment. Her lips opened and closed because she wanted to speak but knew she must not. Shahin also stared. Esther tried to see it anew, as through the eyes of a first-timer.

Where hoards were stable islands amassed by the presence of a dragon, an entrepôt was artificially created by opening six Keeps in a hexagonal pattern all within a mile of each other. The placement of the Keeps fixed the ground to the six anchoring Realms, which meant destructive Brights passed over the entrepôt without damaging it. Each Keep had to be from a separate Realm, which meant an administrative apparatus had developed over time to control ingress, egress, trade, and diplomacy.

A wall ringed the entire entrepôt, six gates set equidistant between the Keeps, each Keep and each gate distinctive. Inside the wall the place looked a bit like a section of a honeycomb, short avenues splitting into more short avenues and triangular open spaces buzzing with movement and color, although from outside she could hear no sound. It was a lovely sight, attractive because it was a haven filled with Realm life and thus survivable, even if survival wasn't necessarily freedom, not here and not anywhere. Paradise remained out of reach. She hadn't glimpsed the burning wings of any guardian angels in all her years traversing the Beyond.

Which abruptly reminded her of the gaoler in Zosfadal's hoard. Why did that gaoler resemble a description of angels from the Tanakh? The wraith in the kitchen had looked an awful lot like a barrow haunt plucked out of a tale she'd read long ago. Was that an accident? Or her Earth-bound biases imposing familiarity on unfamiliar things?

The entrepôt grew harder to see. The twilight was darkening from Gloam into Pitch. They needed to get a move on.

Marianne slid down the tip of the last vertebra to crunch boots to the ground. Faye and Lydia followed her, one with grace and the other with power. Shahin hesitated before reluctantly gesturing toward the foot he limped on.

Lydia made a brace with her hands. Faye extended her staff to act as a railing, and she was strong enough to hold it fast as he clambered down with their assistance, giving a nod of thanks. Without being asked they waited to help Esther. Age took its toll no matter how hard you trained to stay functional. She was grateful for their hands easing the distance, for the staff to hold on to, especially because of the twinge in her ankle when she hit the ground. Someday, sooner than she cared to think, she, too, would have to retire from work she loved rather than risk the others. But not today.

Today she was getting Daniel back.

They stood about a kilometer from the wall. Like a Keep, an entrepôt's steadying influence stretched a distance outward, so while there were crevices in the flat ground between here and the nearest gate, they remained narrow enough to step across. Even so, the Hex had gotten only halfway to the gate when darkness swept down like the wolf on the fold. One moment they jogged in gray twilight and the next the Pitch threw a cloak of darkness over them, forcing the group to stop dead in their tracks lest they stumble and break a leg or trip over something worse.

Esther lit to her full span although she was already worn out. She knew she could not hold for long. It just had to be long enough. The first thing she saw was Gus's insubstantial form gesturing toward the right, signaling with emphatic hand signs: *Warning! Immediate! Danger!*

A massively large creature loomed out of the darkness accompanied by the ticky ticking rhythm of too many hammering legs. This was not an antic swarm. This was far worse.

The monster was the height of a big pickup and so long its back end couldn't yet be seen. It undulated forward on a hundred or maybe a thousand legs. It oozed; it writhed; it opened a maw with a gaping gullet big enough to engulf a horse.

Marianne stopped dead, jerked as if she'd been stung by something in the air, and stumbled backward with a yell, slamming into Lydia. Esther flung out her arms to steady them both. Shahin's gasp sounded more like a curse.

"Don't move," she warned him. "They go after movement."

Faye leaped forward, spinning her staff until its blue light became a glare so sharp that Esther had to shade her eyes. The Shotgun ran straight into the monster's mouth, heedless of its mandibles. The maw convulsed shut, closing up.

Faye was gone.

"Oh god, oh god," whispered Marianne hoarsely.

Shahin took a step forward. "Shouldn't we try—?"

"Wait!" said Esther, knowing how heartless she must sound. "The inside is their only vulnerable part."

The creature halted, as if content now that it had caught its prey. For three breaths a horrible stillness. An impossible dread. Gus had vanished into the darkness seething beyond the monster. A faint hum burned at Esther's ears.

The top of the monster's head shuddered. It shifted, cracked. A splinter of blue light leaked out, followed by a sudden, violent series of cuts that scraped through the carapace. The tip of Faye's staff slashed into view with murderous power. She sliced through with a magic as unyielding as every Shotgun's loyalty. Too late it tried to scuttle backward. The top of its head peeled right off before the body knew it was gone. The forward mass slid sideways and hit the ground with a squalid, squishy thump and a spray of nasty wet drops.

Faye leaped free of the flaccid mouth. The huge body writhed in a reflexive death whip. And just in time! Its hindquarters slammed into a second monster racing close behind. The force caused the second one to tumble into a roll, its hundred legs chopping at the air as it landed on its back, helpless to charge them. Which was a good thing, since they'd never have been able to run fast enough to escape it.

Esther saw Gus's wispy form at last, farther out in the darkness, signaling. At least two more long shapes flowed out of the blackness. The sound of their greasy chittering hit like icy spikes in Esther's ears. She knew better than to freeze, yet her legs felt stuck even as Lydia and Marianne bolted to the left to get out of the way of the oncoming assault.

"Move!" shouted Faye, grabbing Shahin's arm to haul him after her.

Esther found her legs worked after all. She staggered after the others, feeling a presence rise at her back like the tickle of antennae reaching out to find her, to grasp her, to devour her. But no maw closed over her. She looked back.

The monsters circled the body of their dying companion, and closed in to begin crunching and slurping. Food was food, and in the Beyond, easy food was a luxury.

"Esther! Move it! We need your light!" Faye's voice jolted her.

They weren't out of danger yet. The dome of her rapidly shrinking light was their only path across the last half a kilometer to the entrepôt gate. They ran the rest of the way. Faye's red boots stamped moist footsteps, and globules dripped from her coat, which shed the toxins of the Beyond as the oil in a duck's feathers shed water.

The wall rose about twice Esther's height. A brick terrace warned their feet that they had reached the gate. It had no physical door. Instead, its archway shimmered like a pale curtain woven of glittering threads. Marianne cut an opening, and they pressed through one at a time, Gus last of all. The rip sealed with a hiss behind him. He grasped Esther's hand with a reassuring squeeze. Everyone stood a moment in silence, catching their breath. Faye shook a last few droplets off her sleeve, leaving her coat again immaculate.

Finally, as in slow-mo, Shahin reached up, took hold of his sunglasses, slid them down the bridge of his nose to peer over the top at a now physically solid Gus as at a mystery he could not fathom. After a moment, he pulled off the sunglasses entirely to examine the chamber.

The entry area was a triangular room. A long counter separated the space into two halves. They were alone. Esther walked forward to the counter on which sat an old-fashioned bell ringer. Had this entrepôt hired the same interior designers as Zosfadal, with a preference for vintage styles? She pressed the ringer six times, one for each person in the group.

A door slid open. A person ambled out, dabbing their

forehead with a cloth. They had a funneled mouth, feathery ears, and two arms with hands split into elongated fingers. At the counter, the person deftly set out various implements, a ledger, and a tablet that resembled an Etch A Sketch. When everything was arranged as they wanted it, they shrilled a whistle.

Lydia whistled back, then indicated Esther. "The clerk is a Voice and can understand if you speak English."

Esther usually took point in these situations. She wasn't the oldest in her Hex. Gus was two years older, and Lydia had been born in ancient Śfarda. But Esther had been with the Hex the longest of the current configuration and was anyway the bossiest, as Marianne often complained, not without cause. Daniel's father had once told her she was too in love with the idea of righting the wrongs of the multiverse and that sometimes altruism was just selfishness, and he hadn't been wrong. Here she was anyway.

She approached at an unthreatening walk. Entering an entrepôt required a clearance procedure mandated by the Concilium, like passport control. Because they had lost their license Esther had known this part of the expedition was going to be improvisational. She decided to deploy urgency and confidence.

"We seek admittance, as per the greater treaty of trade between Realms. We have been through here before and have no record of mishap, disruptive behavior, or criminal intent in this zone. We seek passage to cross to Elegance Keep. We apply for no license for trade, diplomatic ventures, or negotiations within the zone. We know the route and will quickly move through and be gone."

As required, she set down their Hex badge with its starfish symbol and Concilium-granted freelancer license incised in runes on the back. Next to it she set down a small platinum ring, the standard price of passage into an entrepôt. The clerk picked up the badge and studied the runes for what seemed like five thousand years even though it was perhaps thirty seconds. Then, without further speech, the clerk left the entry chamber through a different door.

"That's not good," muttered Marianne. "We could leave right now and go the long way around."

"How long would it take from here to Dunkirk?" Esther asked.

"We would have to return to the dragon spine and wait for the next Bright to rearrange the Beyond since right now those chasms make it impassable. Then . . ." She trailed off.

"In other words, it could take days. Or weeks. Compared to under an hour if we're allowed to pass. If they refuse us entry, *then* we'll go the long way around. But if you prefer, we can take a vote."

"It's too late to take a vote," retorted Marianne. "The clerk took our badge, or didn't you notice?"

"So we wait," said Lydia, crossing her arms. "We still have gambits. Best options right now seem like Kidnapped or Get Help. And I have a lotus eater in my pack."

"That's what I'm afraid of," retorted Marianne. "I need this new gig I've been offered. Not a prison term in some peninsula hellhole."

Lydia cocked her head with a look of mockery. "Whatever trouble we get in, Esther will gladly take the blame. It's her son we're rescuing. Remember?"

With a snort, Marianne turned her attention to the ledger. She began paging through it as if she hoped to find a record of names and arrivals in a writing system she could read.

Lydia caught Esther's eye and gave a nod made compassionate by the warm sympathy of her gaze. The constant clutching fear that tightened Esther's chest eased a little. Not that the fear for Daniel lessened, but Lydia's support gave her fresh optimism. After the suspension had come down last year, Lydia had departed the next day, leaving only a handwritten note that she needed time to clear her head. So it mattered now to get the message that Lydia still had Esther's back. She needed to hear that, jangled as she was by waiting. As she considered the three gambits Lydia had mentioned, she dug into a vest pocket and pulled out an extra face mask. She tapped Shahin on the arm and handed the mask to him. He asked a question with a quirk of his handsome eyebrows. She mimed pulling the straps on over the head and fixing it to cover nose and mouth. His brow furrowed as he studied the mask, how light and flimsy it must seem.

Faye slid up next to Esther and whispered, "I thought we needed to go to Twin Keep, not Elegance."

"We don't want them to know that."

"Oh." Faye's mouth twitched as she thought it over. "Misdirection."

"Misdirection is an important ally. Are you prepared if we have to use Get Help?"

"I'm kind of hoping we do," said Faye with her brightest smile. Did every Shotgun have this maniacal glee at the thought of mayhem? A rhetorical question.

Esther went over to hug Gus. It was always good to lean on Gus, a big man of few words and a lot of life experience he never spoke about. They'd met in navy ROTC, way way way back in the day, and had been good friends ever since he'd punched a guy who wouldn't take no for an answer at a bar.

"Listen." She kept her voice low so Shahin wouldn't hear.

"It's been five years since the Dunkirk collapse. None of us have been back there. Even if tendrils of stability can cling to the remaining five Keeps, the main part of the settlement will be eroded and changed. It's going to be hard to retrace a path back to where I found Kai. I never even knew what the enterprise's name was. The coordinators just gave me a location and a job to do."

Gus rested a hand on her shoulder. "I've survived multiple clusterfucks. We'll get it done."

Lydia went to the door where the clerk had disappeared and pressed an ear against it. She listened for a while before shaking her head and returning to Esther.

Marianne handled each of the implements the clerk had left behind, examining them as if they were collectibles in an exclusive antique shop. She pointedly did not touch the ring. Shahin prowled a circuit of the chamber, running a hand along the wall as if checking for unseen messages or hidden signals.

The door opened and the clerk hustled in, followed by a squad of goons, in this case Ek'en enforcers wearing uniforms that marked them as agents of the Concilium. They stood twice the height of the clerk and were packed with muscle, sporting claws and tusks that made the long poles with sharpened hooks they carried seem superfluous. Given the Ek'nyanyar Realm's long history of alliance with the dragons one might have thought them all to be typical *minions,* but Esther had allies among an Ek' radical faction who had striking philosophical and political differences with their ruling gentes.

A human-looking individual followed the squad, holding the Hex's starfish badge and a tablet incised with ideograms. This person examined each of them before settling on Esther.

"I am the Voice assigned to this gate. Star of Evening, a year ago your Hex was accused and proscribed by the Concilium for contract infringement. You have violated the terms of your suspension. By order of the Concilium, and in order to prevent you from further violations, your Hex is remanded to Isolaria Prison in the Realm of Ek'nyanyar until your mandated term of suspension is up. This translates into nine more Realm-of-Earth years."

Behind them, the gateway sizzled as magic cut through it from the Beyond. The unknown Hex, the one they'd thought lost to the Bright, tumbled in just in time to see Esther and the others led away under guard.

13

The Ek'en hustled them along a hallway that zigged and zagged through the interior of a large compound. The Voice-in-charge strode at the front, no longer speaking. They passed any number of closed apertures. Some were sliding doors, some latched or knobbed, some set below the ceiling as if for flying or crawling, some too narrow for a human to fit through. It was uncannily quiet, as if soundproofing draped the passages. A gracile Olongi loped past, not looking up from a perusal of a strip of fabric marked with runes and held taut like an emergency message needing to be delivered.

The guards ushered them into a holding area. The entry opened onto a hallway lined with cells. The Voice-in-charge made a clicking noise as prelude to speaking to the Ek'en.

"Lotus," said Esther.

At the rear, Gus casually kicked the big door, as if by accident. The instant it shut, the Hex slipped on masks. Lydia threw a golf-ball-sized sphere hard to the ground. Its thin shell shattered and the impact triggered a spell Daniel had woven, spilling an aerosol mist.

The Ek'en went down fast, eyes glazing over in a dreamy oblivion. Shahin was on his knees before Faye helped him get the mask properly in place. The Voice-in-charge staggered toward a counter, gave a few short blurts of sound, and collapsed onto the floor into a deep sleep. Esther wrested the starfish badge from their appendage.

It took a minute in and out. They left the holding area behind and walked briskly, careful not to run, along empty hallways toward what Marianne assured them was a public exit from the compound. Shahin yawned, shook his head, and blinked a few times as if casting off the dregs of the spell. Once they were far enough away, they pulled off the masks, stowed them, and replaced them with earplugs.

"What's this?" he murmured as Esther handed him a spare set.

"Put one in each ear."

As they reached a big glass door overlooking a large forecourt, Lydia began humming. She couldn't cast sleep or oblivion in the way Daniel's spells could, but she could use her magic to dull awareness. The two guards on duty and the clerk at the entry desk drooped, not looking up as the Hex strode past.

Gus slid aside one of the doors and closed it behind them. They split into pairs as they descended the steps, Lydia with Marianne, Gus with Faye, and Esther with Shahin. Esther tucked her earplugs into a pocket, letting Shahin keep his in case they needed them again. No one shouted after them as they crossed the wide forecourt as seemingly unrelated parties.

Above, a shimmering vault marked the presence of a transparent dome of magical force protecting the entirety of the entrepôt. Gloam had returned in the Beyond, allowing her to see clouds of antics as they swirled on the other side, unable to land. Now and again a shadow of a prowling creature rippled across, although Esther couldn't see its shape, or if it had a fixed shape at all.

A boundary wall enclosed the compound. Past a triple

archway lay the entrepôt's reason for existing. The central zone was a marketplace where people from many Realms exchanged goods and services. A lively blend of sound rose in the air, everything one could ever hope for from a bustling trade zone. Melodic chimes rang amid shouts of laughter. A whistling song was drowned out by the scrape of wheels and the *beat beat beat* of a passing drum. An ocean of hisses and trills, clicks and clacks, plinks and plonks, buzzing, whooping, hammering, the rising and falling rhythm of a multitude of voices.

Esther carefully did not look toward the others, now some distance away, as she and Shahin strode into the bazaar. Any other time she would have reveled in the chance to stroll the streets amid the crowds. She'd have wound a browsing path through narrow back alleys and quaint lanes lined with shops and stalls from so many different miraculous places, because wasn't life in all its wild variety a miracle? Weren't ingenuity and art and craftsmanship miracles of discipline and creativity? The existence of such entrepôts—she knew of eleven and had set foot in seven of them—remained, for her, a constant, joyous marvel. The universe was unimaginably large and yet she could reach out and touch Kai's elbow, could pick up her grandchildren whose forebears on Kai's side arose in unknown regions—*here be dragons*—while they were prosaically human on Daniel's side. Yet stardust made them all. Didn't it?

A hand brushed her arm, startling her into raising an arm defensively. It was Shahin, getting her attention since her mind had been elsewhere. She flexed her hand with an awkward flush, but he didn't seem to notice.

He spoke in a low voice. "Why did we split up from the others?"

"So we'll be harder to track down once the guards wake up."

"I have a lot of questions about what just happened."

"I see I'm rubbing off on you."

He slipped his sunglasses up, ruffling back his hair, and gave her a smile that would have knocked young Esther right over. "Heaven forfend."

A flutter kicked under her breastbone and her cheeks grew warm. She hadn't felt this unreasonably young for years. She'd grown a harder shell by now, although clearly not hard enough. *This is not the time or the place or the person. Absolutely not. No, no, no.*

For once in her life, she could not dredge up a sparkling retort.

"Lotus-eaters appear in the *Odyssey*. They fall asleep." He spoke with a lift of the eyebrows, as if inviting her in on the joke.

She took refuge in explanation because the alternative was to break out in a goofy, infatuated smile and that would never ever do. "They'll sleep about an hour or so. Even if someone stumbles upon them it should take some time to wake them up, untangle the mystery, and send searchers after us. We can reach Twin Keep as long as we don't do anything to look suspicious."

"At the entry gate you said we were going to Elegance Keep."

"I did say that."

"I see." He slid the sunglasses down to hide those brilliant eyes. It was almost a relief.

"Yes. Always sow confusion. This way."

She gestured toward a side street. Overhead a rope of tiny

bells spanned the street's entrance, the ends tied to the roofs of the three-story brick buildings on either side. The bells tinkled as they passed.

"They call this the Street of Bells, for obvious reasons. We are going to go through the garment and fabric district and swing around that way. The others will take different routes. I'm surprised you know about the lotus-eaters. But now that I think about it, I did notice that Zosfadal has a lot of books, so I guess that could include a copy of the *Odyssey*."

"It could."

"If anyone would be a collector, I suppose a dragon would. By why Earth literature?"

"That question is only germane if you are assuming he hoards only Earth literature."

"Huh."

He glanced away, a smile hovering on his lips, then looked back. "I am curious about Augustus Ho. He remained intangible in the oasis but became physical in the hoard and when we reached the entrepôt."

"I guess I didn't explain enough. An oasis is more a part of the Beyond than it is Realm. An entrepôt is more Realm than Beyond. A Realm foothold onto the Beyond, if you will. Six Keeps placed in a hexagonal formation create a kind of super-Keep. If the Keeps all connect to the same Realm, then we call it a peninsula because it is an extension of that Realm. If the Keeps come from six different Realms, then we call it an entrepôt, a trading and diplomatic zone. Like this one."

"People, sentients, of all kinds work here and trade here. Live here, it seems." He gestured to an adult leading several small offspring toward an unknown destination, to damp washing hung from balconies to dry, to a wizened elder buying produce at a corner greengrocer.

"Yes, some live their entire lives in places like this. Peninsulas tend to have a specific political function for their home Realm. Entrepôts develop personalities of their own. Damascus is one of the best, a prosperous and urbane trading city as its namesake on Earth had long been until the war. Here in the Beyond, it is the most welcoming and safest entrepôt, I would say."

"Why is that?"

"Five of the Realms who have Keeps here specifically forbid trafficking in people, so there are no flesh markets. It's why I like doing business here. It's good we're hashing this out now. Once we cross through Twin Keep and reach Dunkirk, we'll be back in the Beyond."

"I'm a bit confused. You and the others have spoken of this place Dunkirk as if it is an entrepôt."

"It used to be. It collapsed because it lost one of its six Keeps. All the Realm-born who were present in the entrepôt when it fell had to flee. That's why my Hex calls it Dunkirk as a shorthand. It's a reference to an event in Earth history when a retreating army was evacuated from a beach."

"Keeps are impossible to destroy."

"That's not quite correct. Keeps are built where a stake has been laid. Stakes are said to be impossible to remove once hammered into place."

"Hammered?"

"A figure of speech. As I understand it, dragons were the first cross-dimensional travelers. They can detect places where Realms brush close up against the Beyond."

"Like an oasis?"

"That's right. My understanding is that a really long time ago they figured out how to stake the two together by means that might be magical or might be a technology an Earth human would perceive as magic. As far as I know, they are the only species who can stake Realms to the Beyond. That's part of what gives them so much power. Anyway, a stake isn't an opening, it's more like an anchor that fixes a point in a Realm to a point in the Beyond. When a Keep is built around a stake, it creates a permanent opening. Think of it as a tunnel between worlds. A tunnel can be flooded or blocked, although not easily."

"What happened at Dunkirk?"

"You ask a lot of questions," she retorted.

He laughed.

Her cheeks warmed. What on heaven and earth indeed? This was absolutely the ridiculously wrong time and it made her angry at herself to get distracted in this way even for an instant when Daniel was a captive and Kai was in danger of being taken from them. And yet why not smile back just for one swift second? "Someday we'll sit down for a long afternoon's coffee at a lovely coffeehouse."

"Will we?" The words fell with a feather's lightness but she felt a weight in them, a meaning she could not fathom.

A blush heated her face. Was she flirting? Was he?

"This way," she said instead of answering. They had to keep moving.

She had been adjusting her pace as they went, speeding up past intersections as if she was headed to a specific stall and then slowing down as if browsing until they turned a convenient corner, when she could speed up again. Shahin's limp was not as pronounced on the even surface of the lanes. They walked for ten minutes in silence; she kept checking her watch. The exchange had left her restless. Her gaze skipped along the shop displays as if her eyes sought an answer, but there were no answers for the questions that had nagged at her longest, some of which she could not even formulate in words. She halted for a full thirty seconds at a particularly colorful and intriguing display of beads arranged by size, color gradient, and shininess.

The merchant was a birdlike individual, aged, frail, and yet keen of eye. They spoke in the simple trade language used by entrepôt merchants. "What is your desire, Gracious One?"

"Alas, Estimable One, I am obliged to an appointment. I have admired too long your exceptional wares. Still . . ."

"You may touch them. They are made from shards of lost Realms washed up on the shore of the Sea of Glass."

Esther brushed her fingers over them, dug a hand in and tipped it sideways so the beads spilled off her palm. Wouldn't the little ones enjoy pouring their hands through a bucket of unearthly beads! Maybe they could touch each one to a tongue and proclaim where it had come from, as Kai had known the scale was from a dragon of the Stone Kindred. Did dragons breed knowledge in their bones or was it learned? Who was Kai anyway? What did she really know about Kai's origins? On the other hand, the babies might just swallow the beads, Joey especially, who would look you right in the eye and do it.

She glanced up, thinking to share the thought with Gus, but of course Gus wasn't with her because he'd gone with Faye. Startled, she realized she was alone.

Shahin no longer stood at her side. He had vanished.

14

She stared up and down the narrow lane and did not see him. What was he thinking to wander off? Would she have to leave him behind as she hurried on to Twin Keep? The thought galled, yet getting Daniel back was the priority. Making sure Kai was safe was the priority.

The merchant clucked. Esther couldn't be sure if the sound was meant in amusement, concern, or criticism of her obvious confusion. "Your companion took the turning into the Street of Garments."

"My thanks, Estimable One. I will return."

"It will be my pleasure to see you again."

She had lost focus. Inattention was a killer. That's how Vincent had died. She could not, would not, lose Daniel or Kai because of her own woolgathering. She fixed her gaze on a post inscribed with ideograms and colored bars and hung with scent bulbs to indicate the beginning of the Street of Garments. No Earth language was represented here. Earth wasn't important enough.

The "street" was a main avenue branching into many lanes and alleys. Esther walked past shops selling chime shirts and decorative tail wraps, third-eye goggles or head coverings to accommodate spiny crests, and the ubiquitous shawls and cloaks woven from fabric as smooth as spring water or as rough as heartbreak. No sign of Shahin on the main drag, but she spotted him down the third lane to the left. Her heart stopped racing so hard.

He stood at a boot stall. As she walked up, he traded his dress shoes for a pair of what looked an awful lot like boondockers. She stole a glance at his stockinged feet to see if there was any obvious reason for the limp. There wasn't.

Boots in hand, he turned to face her. The sunglasses were propped up on his head as a courtesy toward the merchant.

"Nice boots," she said lightly.

He took a few steps away for privacy between stalls, out of earshot. Setting down the rucksack, he winced as he slid his foot into a boot. Speaking to the ground, he said, "My apologies, Esther Green."

She examined him. "What are you trying to tell me?"

He straightened. His hand went to the sunglasses, but he paused. A decision tensed his eyes. He lowered the hand and looked at her without the screen of the lenses. She was tall, and he was about the same height, as slender as a younger man but with the wry, weary humor of a person who has seen much more than he ever wanted to see. He had lovely eyes, damn him, meltingly sweet.

He hooked fingers under his tunic and pulled out the tie. She hadn't realized he was still wearing it. His set expression, the sense he was pushing against a heavy weight, kept her from commenting as he carefully untied and drew it off. Then he opened his hand. The tie dropped to the ground as if by accident but, of course, it was not.

He said quietly, almost triumphantly, "I am a poet."

She swayed as the truth slammed into her. "You're leaving. That's why all those questions about traveling in the Beyond.

About properties of Realms and if people live in entrepôts. You're . . . escaping the boss."

"Perhaps I will say I am liberating myself. My brief time with you and your Hex has been instructive, Star of Evening."

"How will you survive?"

"Poets have asked themselves that question for as long as they have composed their verses, have they not? By one means or another."

"What of Zosfadal?"

"Do you mean to march me back to him against my will?" She caught a laugh in her chest, making a heartfelt grunt as if she'd been struck a friendly bull's-eye. "You know I will not. Does that mean you were not after all his loyal lieutenant?"

"Perpetual service was his only task. But in the end, he would not bow."

The sentiment sounded familiar, even biblical, but she had no time. "What message shall I give him?"

"Do not claim I assaulted your Hex and escaped thereby. The boss will never believe such a tale. Say I told you I had other business and went my way. Then he can puzzle out the truth. One boon I ask of you." He waved fingers to indicate the ground where the tie lay like a flattened snake in a curling heap. "Take the garment into the Beyond and leave it there. What do you wish for in exchange for this task?"

"I will do it freely, without obligation."

"Then you have my thanks."

"I accept them, although thanks are also a form of debt. I would ask you in your turn to help others as you are able." She sighed, not sure how to proceed, reluctant to walk away, and yet she had no time to waffle or drag it out, so it was better to make the parting sharp and clean. "If there is anything you can tell me that would help, I would appreciate the knowledge. For example, the identity of the enterprise who the boss dealt with in this matter, and what he traded for the youth."

"The enterprise marks itself with a trident foot. A three-pronged claw. They deliver rare and one-of-a-kind goods. To the boss, specifically, they deliver books."

"*Books?* Like all those books he has in his hoard?"

"He collects the last and the lost."

"I don't understand why he didn't just return the books and be quit of the debt."

"Because he could not."

"He traded them on to someone else . . . ?"

"He ate them."

The deadpan statement made her laugh. "He ate them? Is that an inside joke?"

"No. He ate them."

Poor Zosfadal, lacking the ability to delay gratification, although eating books sounded like a possible neurosis. No wonder the dragon was desperate. How would you even explain that to your dissatisfied trading partner? Or the Concilium, if it came asking? It put a whole new spin on the idea of devouring a book.

Shahin went on. "I came to be, to what you would call consciousness, in the hoard."

"You have amnesia about your life before?" She had no idea what this had to do with the books, but she knew enough to let him say what he wanted to say because for some reason he thought this was important enough to tell her.

"I know no other place these eyes have seen but I know of other places. How can that be? In the hoard, I am not alone among the residents in living with this conundrum. That is the riddle of our existence. But your time here is almost up, Star of Evening. I will hold you no longer. I offer my farewell. May you be successful."

He was right. She had to go.

"May you be successful, Shahin."

Her feet already shifted to race onward to Twin Keep, to meet the others, to brave what she must to get her son back. An impulse struck hard in her flinty heart. She fished out the other key to the Keep. Pressing it into his fingers, she said, "This will bring you to Daniel's Keep, if you ever need a safe haven."

At the head of the lane a guard patrol halted. They hadn't yet looked this way.

She caught the gaze of the boot seller, eyes with the gleam of bronze. Brighter streaks flickered across them as the merchant looked toward the patrol and casually stepped aside to allow her and Shahin to slide through the stall. A curtain concealed what lay behind the display of boots cut for a variety of weight-bearing appendages.

The poet had one boot unlaced and the other not yet on. Seeing a bench set at the back of the curtained-off area of the stall, he sat. With a flick of a hand he waved Esther to go on. And so she must. She shifted the curtain aside to push past.

He spoke just loud enough for her to hear. "God's mercy surpasses gold and silver. It is greater by far than treasure."

One last meeting of eyes before the curtain slipped down behind her, and he was gone, left behind. She hesitated for one breath, feeling a powerful stab of regret, a sense that she had let go of something she ought not to give up so easily. But there was no time. She set her face forward and strode down a shaded boardwalk that ran along the front of a three-story building. Where it ended, a tiny gap separated it from the next building. She hurried into an alley lined by humble doors, some closed and some open to glimpses of shoemakers and leatherworkers, a line of people waiting for water at a courtyard well, a dim establishment where folk ate and drank accompanied by the delicate lure of a lute, a schoolroom where youths recited in repetitive hoots and whistles and clicks.

She emerged onto a lane whose stalls and shops sold gloves and other coverings for non-weight-bearing appendages. No sign of the patrol. No entrepôt-wide alarms or street closures that would mean guards were on alert and spreading out to find them.

In seven minutes she reached Twin Keep with its twin symbol that looked to Esther's eyes like a pair of serpents intertwined as a caduceus, although Lydia assured her the symbol should properly be loosely translated as the mirror of truth and falsehood and represented a concept rather than an object. Small plazas fronted each Keep, the outer area crammed with food stalls and last-minute supply shops. The Keep's forecourt was a semicircular terrace where a half dozen guards oversaw the line to enter. The guards slouched with boredom. One yawned. It seemed no alert had gone out yet.

That wasn't the only way fortune favored them. The line waiting to enter the Keep consisted only of a single group waiting its turn at the opaque arch. To her surprise, it was the Hex from the oasis, faces still hidden by their distinctive scarves.

She looked around for the others. By a falafel stand at the outer edge of the plaza, Lydia stood as if patiently waiting in line. A classic hidden-in-plain-sight maneuver.

A large figure slipped in beside Esther.

"Thought you got lost," murmured Gus. "Where's Sunglasses?"

"He liberated himself."

"Liberated himself?"

"Took off on his own."

"Nevah see dat coming. You an easy mark, das why." He grinned. "He figured you wouldn't stop him."

"Thanks for the vote of confidence."

"Jus sayin'." His grin faded. "What if this is some kind of trap on the part of the boss?"

"If it is, I'm having a hard time figuring out what it accomplishes."

Gus nodded. "Shahin wouldn't be the first lieutenant to bolt a bad situation."

"As you would know, my old friend."

"Your oldest friend, and nevah forget it. So how will his loss affect the mission?"

"I have one of Zosfadal's scales, so we don't need him to get back to the hoard. I learned two things from him. The boss got books in exchange for Kai. And then he ate the books."

"He ate 'em?"

"That's what Shahin said."

Gus chuckled. "So ono."

"Pretty weird, if you ask me."

"If true, it means he's in a debt he cannot clear."

"That's right. The enterprise he traded with has the mark of a trident foot. That ring a bell?"

"A trident is a pretty standard symbol."

"Yeah. I feel we've seen a mark like that before. One of Daniel's ledgers has a list of all Concilium-approved enterprises and their marks but we've got no way to access that right now." She tilted her head toward Twin Keep's entrance. "What do you make of the Hex there? Are they following us?"

"Well, now, what they are is an interesting story. They're holding a place for us."

"For us? Why would they do that?"

"An exchange of favors. After you warned them. One good deed deserves an answer. Also, their Ghost is human. A marine."

"Are you kidding me?"

"Swear to God. A nice Filipino kid with family in Waipahu, though he grew up in the Bay Area. Well, not a kid anymore. He just seems young to me. No longer active duty. The only Earther in that Hex."

"I see you had time to talk story. Is there a plan—"

A harsh crackle split the air from the direction of Elegance Keep. Esther and Gus exchanged glances. Faye peeked out from where she crouched in the lee of a food cart. From the line, Lydia looked Esther's way and tilted her head toward the Keep.

The guards stiffened to alertness, and three broke away to run toward the main avenue that led toward Elegance Keep. Esther and Gus headed out as one toward Twin Keep. Faye fell in behind, Lydia coming after her. One of the remaining guards glanced toward them as they approached but there was nothing suspicious about the casual way they were all walking, and naturally the guards were more concerned with whatever commotion was going on at the other Keep, out of their sight.

The four converged to reach Twin Keep at the same time. There were six of the other Hex members with heads wrapped and concealed, not five. Had they picked up a Cargo? No, the sixth was Marianne, pretending to be one of them.

"Good timing," Marianne murmured, indicating the entry.

The archway into Twin Keep changed color from an opaque gold to a shimmering amber translucence, a sign the Keep could be entered by the next group in line. The other Hex's Gate held open the arch as Esther and her people hurried into the archway. A shout rang out from a distance, something about closing all the entries, trouble, an illegal intrusion.

But the rest of her Hex was already through. The transition snapped through Esther's flesh as she crossed last. She, Gus, Lydia, Faye, and Marianne were all inside, still in one piece and still moving.

Marianne tugged down the scarf to reveal her face. "Where's Sunglasses?"

"Nu! We're headed on."

Unlike their modest home Keep, tucked into a banyan tree, the interior of Twin Keep was a train station, although in this Realm the trains were living creatures.

At the customs counter a Keeper lounged resplendent in a glass bowl set on a large tripod. From this height the Keeper watched over four clerks. One clerk's counter cleared as a party of merchants pushed through an opened barrier. Past the counter's entry aisles lay a concourse and ramps leading to terminals from which a traveler could grab a train to anywhere in the Home-of-Honorable-Heaven, which was how Lydia translated the name of this Realm. Everyone in a Schedule Six Realm knew about the Beyond and might think to travel to an entrepôt as part of their work, mercantile interests, education, or whim. The echoing concourse sang of amazing vistas to visit, unknown landscapes, adventure, strange sights and stranger companions.

Faye glanced toward the concourse that lay beyond the counters. She'd never been through here before, and after this fiasco who knew if she'd ever have a chance to return. But Esther led them away from the counters. They weren't here to pass through customs into the Realm. Instead they walked parallel to the counters and into a darkened lobby. At one end of the lobby, bumble hives lit the interior of a small, transparent geodesic dome, one of the Concilium agencies that supervised the heavy traffic in and out of Schedule Five and Six Realms. Agents looked busy with paperwork inside, no one looking up.

Twin Keep was two Keeps built so close together they shared the lobby. For reasons known only to dragons, two separate stakes had been placed unusually close together, anchoring two wildly separated points in the Beyond. The Damascus-linked Keep belonged to the xkievo-cerulean-sweet federation. The Dunkirk-linked Keep was subject to the ipsovr-sandstone-umami federation.

They hurried into an entry foyer and past a silent customs counter into an abandoned portage hall. The ipsovr federation was one of the entities that licensed what was commonly referred to as flesh traffic, the cartage and sale of sentient species between Realms. With the collapse of Dunkirk, regular trade through this entrepôt had ceased. Disruption had been the whole point of the action, and it had worked.

Amid the mercifully empty cages and posts to which captives had once been chained, only one light was lit. A slouched Keeper sat half tipped out of a shallow bowl, leaning over a tray. A companion sat on the other side of the tray.

They played a game that apparently involved snatching tiny scuttling creatures off a shifting surface and eating them.

Hearing footsteps, the Keeper looked up. The companion shut the tray, sliding a lock onto the lid, and slipped away to fade into the shadows. The Keeper settled back into the molasses-thick liquid of its bowl. Fore-tentacles whipped out a series of splashes across the liquid.

Lydia said drily, "The Honorable-of-Heaven Washed-In-Happenstance-Joy recognizes you, Esther, from last time we were through here. Good tidings! They want nothing to do with you."

"Does that mean we can go through?"

The Keeper made a noise suspiciously like musically insulting flatulence.

Lydia raised both hands, palms up, with a shrug. "I won't translate. The honorable won't interfere and won't ask questions."

Esther kept walking toward a passage terrace placed at the farthest forward point of the chamber. The air smelled of something like mothballs, as if it hadn't been aired out in five years. Their footsteps echoed. This hall had once been a bustling hive of trade in and out of an entrepôt made prosperous by misery. A fierce surge of satisfaction coursed through her. Her allies had crippled the small link in a bigger chain that Dunkirk entrepôt represented. Whatever else her life had been—and losing Vincent to that stupid accident ten years ago had made her question the point of it all—her part in the operation counted for something.

The Hex reached the terrace and lined up at what appeared to be a smooth blank wall: the crossing point. Yet as Marianne opened a gate, as Gus slipped through to scout ahead, as they waited for his return, she knew that people, sentient individuals both captive and free, had died because of the sabotage. Their deaths begged the inevitable question: Was it worth it?

Yet was there ever a time that an unjust system would cease to exist without a struggle? Did any entrenched institution ever apologize and retire gracefully to open the ground for something new, maybe better, maybe worse? And so it goes.

Gus was gone longer than expected. Faye kept her attention on the light that marked the Keeper behind them, sweeping the dark hall with her vigilant gaze. No one troubled them, although they heard someone or something moving around in the shadowed chamber, something that never showed itself, if it was even there and not a sound bleeding through from the Realm.

Esther's palms felt sweaty. She licked her lips. All rested on what lay ahead. How was Daniel doing? Was Zosfadal treating him as a respected Keeper? She had to cling to the thought that Zosfadal would act with self-interest and not harm his captive. It was a struggle not to spin into panic. What if she was wrong about Shahin and he was really part of a clever plan to attack the empty Keep while she and the others were gone, to grab Kai? She had given Shahin a key, for goodness' sakes!

No. These were mind gremlins spinning out of control. Without a Keeper inside, a Keep was essentially barred and barricaded from the Beyond, even with a key to bring you to the foot of the tower.

Gus still had not returned. Faye shifted her staff to her other hand. Marianne rubbed her face with one hand as she held open the gate with the other. Lydia stood with eyes closed, listening. A whisper chased through from the other side, maybe a wind off the Beyond, maybe alien speech.

Esther ran a hand over her hair, brushed a few stray curls off her forehead. Were Kai and the babies all right? Would she find the information she needed? Would she be able to engineer a solution? No, that couldn't be a question. She would. She must.

Gus reappeared, looking grim. He gave a throat-cutting gesture to Marianne. Surprised, she released the tear. With a hiss, the opened seam melded back together.

He said, "Conditions are okay. Gloam, a bit on the heavy side of twilight but not in apparent transition and no immediate clouds or monsters for at least one hundred yards out."

"But?" asked Esther, Lydia, and Marianne at the same moment.

He shook his head with a grimace. "There's a lot of rubble, and people are living there. Like a shantytown. The ground has a funky bedrock feel."

"There are five Keeps still left, like this one," said Esther.

"Maybe that's why people have risked setting up shop."

Faye spoke without turning, keeping her gaze on any possible threats from the hall. "Realm folk can't survive in the Beyond."

Esther said, "They can if they can get supplies, are willing to fight constantly, and have figured out a way to protect themselves against the Bright."

Gus added, "There's still something different about this."

"Is there any obvious obstacle between us and the area where Kai was being held?" Esther asked.

"I don't think so."

"I'd rather hear a no, but I'll settle for a think so."

"I miss Sunglasses," said Marianne. "Where'd he go, anyway? Him and that expensive suit and shoes. Whew."

"I didn't ask."

"He said he was bolting, eh? No wonder you and your bleeding heart didn't ask." Marianne's lip curled. Esther braced herself. "Nah, I'd love to keep sniping, but there isn't time. The sooner we go, the sooner we get it done, and I'm ready to be done."

Esther caught her eye and held it. "You'll stay here, at the entrance to the Keep."

Marianne stiffened. "Don't you trust me?"

"That's the point, Mar. I'm leaving you as backup in case things go pear-shaped and we need to be able to get out as quickly as possible. Once we go into the ruins you can leave and we'd be stranded. I trust you not to do that."

Marianne was silent for a few breaths. "God knows you and your righteous crusades annoy me. Sorry, Chava once informed me in that way she has that I shouldn't say *crusade* since you're not Christian, but you know what I mean. Anyway, thanks for the vote of confidence."

Esther allowed herself a moment to imagine Chava's tone, and the amusement she felt made it easier to take Marianne for who she was, with all her complicated aspects both good and not so good. "You're the best Gate I know."

"How many Gates do you know? One?" Marianne's sardonic humor had appealed to Esther at their first meeting. It had been a long time since Esther had seen it.

"Listen, I know the path I've taken the Hex on has rubbed wrong for you. I can't blame you, since you signed up for something else, and it's gotten between us. I will always respect your skills and your work."

Marianne's shoulders relaxed although the sarcastic curl

of her lips sharpened. "I do need your signature to release me early, so you're in luck. I'll wait."

It was as close as Marianne would ever come to giving someone a sentimental hug.

"There you have it," said Esther. "Let's go."

15

A seamless transition catapulted them from the musty air of the portage hall into a cool twilight glamor. They were back in the Beyond.

Dunkirk had been about the same physical area as Damascus, the maximum possible for an entrepôt. Like Damascus it had been built on a hexagonal grid system but with more barriers on its streets to control movement, more cages and pens, more suspicion and more suffering. Now the barriers and walls and trading compounds were rubble, not as if bombed or earthquaked or slammed with wrecking balls, but as if, every time a Bright poured through, its heat or ice had collapsed many of the buildings, softened stone and brick, and twisted and molded the remains turn by turn into barely recognizable ruins. Yet the footprint of the former town was there, a foundation impossible to obliterate.

And why should that be? What was holding it together?

Smoke hung in the air, mixing with tendrils of an eel-like living mist she'd seen only in the Beyond. The entrepôt had been flat. Now, hillocks pushed up here and there. What she could see in the twilight looked like a blanket rumpled into erratic folds. Avalanches of bricks and roof tiles created shoals and reefs on lower ground.

More startlingly, there was light.

Light! Not an approaching Bright but steady bulbs that might be powered by electricity or oil or some other luminescent substance. At the crest of a distant hillock rose the sabotaged Keep. It resembled an inkblot coniferous tree, backlit by the Gloam. What looked like floodlights ringed the broken Keep. A fence of yet more lights ran down the hill, acting as a barrier close to the ground, while strings like holiday lights ran up and down half-melted walls below. Fires burned on open hearths. The sight shocked her. Yet it made sense. The creatures of the Beyond avoided light.

The sound of voices and life, more than she would have imagined, drifted through the air. Off to their right a shape moved, disappearing through a gap in a wall. A creature of the Beyond would have swarmed toward them, insatiably attracted by the fierce energy of Realm existence. Was this a sentry going to alert whoever was in charge? Was someone in charge? She thought of pirate havens and bandit hideouts, then forced herself to clear her thoughts of expectations and assumptions. Those would kill you, especially in this line of work.

Marianne had already closed the gate. Seated with her back to the Keep she set a machete across her thighs, a thermos to her left, and waved at them. Gus picked a path through twisted layers of rubble. Trade compounds that had once risen like unassailable forts were now little more than outlines along the ground to mark how rooms had been laid out. The generous expanse of spacious audience chambers and opulent living quarters for the masters and dealers contrasted with rows of tiny cells for the trafficked.

They made their way along what remained of old streets. Unlike Damascus, with its central marketplace open to all,

Dunkirk had been territorial, each section separated from the others by its own security and passage requirements. If Twin Keep were twelve o'clock, the compound they wanted had been situated at about nine, halfway between the western edge and the center. The Hex moved with cautious but determined speed, working their way around and inward. Gus scouted out the best line as they advanced.

Faye gave a hand signal: they were being followed. Gus's expression tightened. He vanished within broken walls and hazy twilight.

Esther spotted the metal superstructure of the infamous foundry where so many chains had been welded. Stark anger flared at seeing it again. Its glass roof was gone but its shell appeared unaltered, an ominous metal scaffolding whose highest girders were hard to see in the twilight. It was a place that could easily rise again to manufacture yet more shackles, in whatever form they took.

The compound she was looking for had stood in a district on the other side of the foundry's chimneys. They could walk the long way around the huge network of foundry buildings on what remained of the streets, or they could go through.

Taking the lead, she moved into the foundry, past cold furnaces, empty molds, shattered crucibles. Lydia stayed a few steps behind with Faye at the rear. An eerie quiet chased them. Mist drifted in pillars like the disintegrating shapes of forgotten people who had once labored here, some willingly and many against their will.

A blaze of triumph flared in Esther's heart. She had helped destroy this. It was only one place, this was only one trading zone, but even if you couldn't save every starfish beached by an unexpected tide, it mattered to the ones you could save. It had mattered here, not just for Kai and what Kai had come to mean to her family, but to the other imprisoned ones who had fled. Had they run to freedom or into another servitude or into death? Of such unanswered and unanswerable questions was the world made, and thus its comforts would always be incomplete and temporary.

Her boot stubbed a hard object. She bent and picked up a broken link of chains.

Each small individual act was part of a greater community of movement.

A scuff alerted Esther. Faye hurried to stand beside her.

Out of a smear of darkness walked five people with the skulk of ruffians. One held a burning lantern while the others carried bladed weapons intended, she thought, to represent some aspect of a Hex's parts: a pole-arm, a cleaver, twin swords, and a crossbow. None carried the magic of a Hex. She felt its lack as an instability in their formation. The ruffians paused as they looked over the newcomers, sensing their own weakness. They wore fake Hex badges marked with a three-pronged claw. The trident foot. *Aha*.

Gus came up behind the other group, unheard, weaving through their ranks. As they realized he was there, they jumped, startled by his ghostly arrival. One even swung a sword at him but the blade passed through air. Faye stamped forward and lowered her staff into fighting stance. The blue glow limned its length as she called magic into the haft. Esther flipped her multi-tool's lightning rod out, infusing it with light.

The silence dragged on. No one moved.

Esther nodded at Lydia.

The Voice spoke in a low tone infused with a threatening rumble. "I'd go now, while you still can walk."

The ruffians retreated together into the darkness, but they looked prudent, not scared.

"They don't want an open fight where I have room to maneuver," murmured Faye, then clapped a hand over her mouth.

Esther moved. They wouldn't have much time because the others were likely to regroup and make a new plan.

The far wall of the foundry was mostly intact, its big double doors stuck as if welded shut, but there was a gap in the wall, a hole melted through it. Gus ducked into view and gave them the all clear. They trotted several blocks along a street until they reached the compound she had ever after thought of as Vile House. The alliance leaders hadn't told her the name of the enterprise, only which district and compound she was assigned to for the operation. Her part had been to enter a compound before zero hour and to find and release prisoners at the signal. It was a modest if perilous task compared to the grueling and dangerous engineering job needed to block the targeted Keep. She needed mostly the ability to walk into a big room populated by suspicious clerks, ambitious lieutenants, and a big boss, all while keeping a poker face and a relaxed demeanor.

Curiously, the outer walls of the compound had remained intact. She recognized the entrance's triple arches carved to represent a night sky. Three moons and a winged humanoid spanned the apex of each arch. Each humanoid bore the enterprise's symbol on their chest: a three-pronged claw. The trident foot.

Just as Shahin had said.

She'd forgotten, or perhaps not noticed because it hadn't been important to her task at that time. The presence of the ruffians suggested the trident foot enterprise was still operating here via unofficial channels and through its own gang of unlicensed enforcers. Huh.

Lydia nudged her with an elbow and lifted expressive eyebrows. *Time's a-wasting,* that look said.

Esther led them in, just as she had five years ago, only it had been Trey instead of Faye as their Shotgun then. He'd been eager, maybe too eager, and she regretted what had come after because of the injuries he had taken. But that was water under the bridge. Set emotion aside. Yet entering now triggered memories of entering then, until she felt doubled, the Esther of five years ago walking alongside the Esther of today.

The receiving hall had lost most of its roof. It looked rather like an old monastery church eroded until only walls remained. They crunched across broken roof tiles scattered across what had been a beautiful mosaic floor depicting the flora and fauna of a hundred Realms. She had walked along that floor in clean boots, once upon a time, marveling at its workmanship and wondering if it was a shopping list of precious, valuable items. She had waited in a line with others waiting to speak their business to the august representatives of the enterprise. Poker face. Relaxed demeanor. Nothing that might give away her expectation of the imminent destruction of Tree Keep and the collapse of the entrepôt.

The memory of the explosion, the moment Tree Keep had lost its connection to the entrepôt, was still visceral, felt in her body more than in her mind. A strong tremor had shaken the ground. The magic of joined Keeps had imploded like air being sucked out of her lungs back into the Realms. Terrified shouts and screams had exploded all around, people running, pushing, shoving, trampling, and fighting as they raced to get to a Keep and into the safety of a Realm.

There was a cost to sabotage. She knew it and she was guilty of agreeing to it. But there had been no hope of gradual rapprochement, no changing of minds, no treaty, no future agreement to be worked toward. One blocked Keep dissolved the hexagon that created stable ground. In an instant, it was doomed.

After the explosion she'd pushed against the frantic outward flow, worming her way inward. She'd shoved her way past panicked people escaping the many offices, had made her way into the heavily walled and guarded back lot of the compound. By then all the enterprise members had fled.

She followed the route she had taken then. Now the empty offices looked frozen in time, furniture in place as if clerks had stepped out for a spot of lunch. How odd that across five Earth years the Bright hadn't altered these rooms for as many times as it must have swept through.

Gus was right. Something was strange here.

In the back half of the compound stood the warehouses with their valuables, some of the doors still barred and bolted, but she wasn't here for material objects. On the day of the attack she, Lydia, and Trey had run past the warehouses to the prison block, the one with a locked entrance door that her multi-tool burned through in eight excruciatingly long seconds.

When they reached the door now, it still stood open, dust accumulated at its base. Cautiously they proceeded down the long dark passageway, Esther's light illuminating their path. Every cell door was ajar, everything left as it had been abandoned on that terrible day.

Even the guards had run on that day, wanting only to save themselves. It had been easy to open all the cells and cages. She'd volunteered the Hex for this specific job, with their consent. She'd known the risks of what she did: She could be injured or killed by a frightened captive who saw her as a threat, driven to desperation by abuse and fear. Or someone in the audience hall might remember her and later link up her presence with the act of sabotage—as, eventually, Zosfadal had.

Back then she'd opened each cell and gone on to the next. Behind her, Trey had coaxed people out, given them a token, and pointed them toward the exit, where Lydia waited with directions. In the end they couldn't be sure how many had reached any of the refugee networks the alliance had set in place. Some of the networks had later collapsed or been shut down by the Concilium. People vanished into the Concilium's prisons or into hiding or death or new servitude or despair.

On the day of the collapse, she had reached the back of the prison block to find a protected guards' room with various surveillance paraphernalia and three double-doored closets, their doors thrown open to reveal hooks where weapons could be hung. The weapons were gone, and the guards had fled through a heavy door that led directly outside. Esther had had one foot over the door's threshold, headed out to see if there were other buildings behind this one, when an instinct halted her. Maybe it was a whiff of air that hinted of musty, damp tunnels. Maybe it was a still, small voice whispering that she hadn't yet completed the task. Because one double-doored closet had not been opened, its doors still locked. She had burned out the lock and tugged open its doors to reveal a flight of stairs.

"Esther, are you all right?" Lydia came up beside her, although back then Lydia had never come this far into the prison block. The Voice nudged her with concern, then saw the stairs. "Blessed gods preserve us, what is down there?"

They stood now before the same closet doors, stuck open on broken hinges. Esther was sure she hadn't broken them that day. The stairs descended into an oily darkness that seemed alive. Impossible to get through. Too dangerous to enter. Best to back away. There is nothing down here but death and despair.

Lydia murmured, "Every cell in my body is screaming to run away."

Faye stepped up to Esther's other side, riding shotgun. "Is that a repulsion spell? My training cohort had a drill where we had to run through them to get to the other side. We called it the chicken drill."

Lydia snorted. Faye's comment lightened the weight, as intended. Maybe back then Esther had been so hyper-focused she'd recognized the dread for the repulsion spell it was, or maybe she hadn't noticed at all and just got on with it, knowing she had limited time, she and the Hex needing to get clear before the Concilium's agents swept in to investigate the collapse. They couldn't afford to be interrogated in the aftermath.

Time was still a-wasting. Esther lit a pale aura and started down, Lydia and Faye behind her. Clammy fingers reached out of the darkness to strangle them . . . but then they pushed through and the spell popped back into place like a taut curtain behind them. Back then, she had counted the steps going down in case she needed that information coming back up. Five years later she recalled the number. After thirty-three steps, the stairs dead-ended on an unlit landing with a final locked door.

16

The door of the last and the lost, she thought now, remembering Shahin's words in the market. She knew for sure she hadn't closed it behind her that day. Someone had been down here since then.

Esther set a hand on the latch and could not hear or sense anything beyond the door's blank opacity. Raising her other hand to alert her companions, she turned the latch and opened the door. It was like stepping into the past.

Behind the door lay a circular shaft of a room lit by a sickly pale light. On a low plinth in the center knelt a wretched young man dressed in a ragged shift, upper arms ringed by shining circles. Head bowed, ankles and wrists shackled to an iron bar bolted into a stone floor. He raised his head and looked her straight in the eye.

No, there was no one on the plinth. The memory had hit with such force that for an instant she had seen his slender frame, the resignation in his eyes, the story of betrayal written through his hopeless expression. But Kai was on Oahu, safe. The circular chamber was empty except for the chains, the iron bar, and an apothecary's cabinet. All its tiny drawers had been pulled out and tossed to the floor. There was a smear of ashy remains where whatever had been in the drawers had been burned and the ashes swept up and taken away.

Faye picked up a tally stick that had gotten wedged against the wall and forgotten. She held it in Esther's light and they examined it.

Esther said in a low voice, "A transaction receipt. Here's the trident foot of Vile House. They trade under the flag of the ipsovr federation. I don't recognize anything else. Lydia?"

The Voice pointed to a symbol that looked something like a superposition of three sine waves. "Over the last year, besides theater work, I've been doing research for the gray market. This is the trade logo of an Earth-based commerce company, a mercenary company, really. It hires out Hexes for transport work through the Beyond. They are on a Concilium surveillance list because they've been linked to illegal trade but never caught at it. Here's proof. These ideograms say they delivered a dragon's 'egg' which can also mean a juvenile, which can mean any dragon under a hundred years old because they're slow to reach what we'd call puberty."

Faye whistled. "The Concilium forbids the transport of dragons, dragon eggs and juveniles, and any dragon effluvia or remains by any Hex. That's the second thing my cohort was taught."

Esther traced the writing burned into the tally stick. "Does this stick refer to Kai?"

"It might be a different dragon's egg. I can't tell. The kindred identifier is burned away."

"If the enterprise was trafficking dragons that would explain this hidden, buried chamber to stay out of Concilium oversight. It sure seems Zosfadal traded with a humanoid faction of slavers to get Kai in the first place, and then traded

Kai on to Vile House, a humanoid enterprise. He must know it's forbidden." She frowned and glanced back toward the open door. "Did you hear something?"

Faye glided to the door, stationing herself to look out without being seen. Her shoulders relaxed as Gus ghosted in and gave a thumbs-up.

"What exactly are we looking for?" Lydia asked. "I'm guessing they burned all the tally sticks to hide illegal trading activity. And whatever else was in these drawers."

"Doesn't it strike you as odd that Kai was here, in the compound, but the enterprise told Zosfadal they never had Kai? What if we are the only witnesses that Kai was delivered as promised?"

"You're the only witness that you found Kai in this compound, and in this chamber," said Lydia.

The words fell like stones. *The only witness.*

Pieces of the puzzle shifted with glacial slowness.

Lydia had been at the front exit of the prison block. Trey had been herding frightened captives down the corridor to the Voice. Marianne's job had been to Gate at one of the Keeps to move people quickly out of the entrepôt. Gus had been assigned with other Ghosts to patrol the outer ring of the zone to warn against the inevitable arrival of antic clouds and monsters.

Esther had come alone down the stairs. She alone had found and unlocked Kai. She'd led Kai up the stairs and, instead of exiting out through the prison block past Lydia and Trey, had fled straight out the open door in the guards' room. There hadn't been another building in the back, just a courtyard stacked with bricks and lined with rubbish bins. Then there had been a powerful ground tremor. A section of the back wall had fallen. Kai had panicked and climbed over the shifting rubble to get out of the compound. She'd followed, and it was there Gus and the others had found them.

She'd been outside of the Vile House compound on a ruptured street calming a traumatized person who they hadn't yet known was a dragon because at no point had Kai shifted from the form she had perceived as that of a young man. Much later he'd told her he had once been able to shapeshift, as some dragons could, but had lost the power to do so after he'd been sold into the hands of slavers, after they'd burned the tattoo-like rings onto his arms. She had no reason to disbelieve him. He had the whirling eyes and mesmer gaze of a dragon and a vast weight of fluid power rippling beneath the surface of an otherwise seemingly unremarkable human body. She couldn't be sure if he had used a dragon's magic that day to convince her to take him with her, and by now it no longer mattered and she wasn't sure he even remembered past the trauma.

Faye's question swam to the surface of her tangled thoughts.

Isn't cross-species reproduction impossible?

She had only ever asked once, when he and Daniel had announced the impending births. Kai had said, with a teasing laugh but serious eyes, that a kwo like him could breed across species. She'd wondered if he was joking since she'd never heard that reproduction with non-dragons was a characteristic of dragons. If anything, dragons normally avoided fraternization of any kind with humanoids. Daniel had later told her, quietly, that it was an upsetting subject for Kai, so she'd never asked again because why would you make that kind of demand of someone you loved?

If she was the only witness, did that mean the enterprise had lied to Zosfadal about not receiving his payment because they thought no one knew Kai had been delivered as promised before the collapse? Or that she'd rescued Kai before they'd known about the delivery?

From the door, Faye rapped her staff sharply on the ground in warning. A metallic clatter rattled from the top of the steps.

Lydia whispered, "Ears up."

Esther slid in her earplugs. She doused her light and moved to the door to peer past Faye's shoulder. Above, a flickering light revealed humanoid forms. They set down a pair of large cages and opened the wire doors with sticks in order to stand well back. Writhing shapes oozed out. Mercifully she could not hear the staccato *click click clack* of a hundred feet ticking and tumbling down the steps but she sure felt it. They were small centipedes, only a foot across and maybe twelve feet long, but deadly all the same and faster and far more agile than their giant brethren.

Faye jumped out to give herself space on the landing, staff raised to point up the steps. She exhaled slowly and, on an inhale, drew on the most exhausting form of a Shotgun's magic. A blue aura limned her body while the staff spat sparks. She wouldn't be able to hold this level for long.

Esther still had the boss's scale but it would mean leaving Marianne. "Gus, warn Mar. Alert the Concilium agents we saw in the concourse. Tell them about the dragon egg tally stick. That'll bring them in. We need backup."

He nodded grimly, then ran up the stairs as the creatures slithered down past him. They paid no attention to him. The humanoids cut at him as he raced past but they could not touch him.

Esther opened the lightning rod of her multi-tool. She

wasn't much of a blade fighter but she could sting. She stepped out to flank Faye.

Behind them Lydia stamped in warning, once, twice, thrice, felt through the stone. She hooted sharply, air expelled as a force pushing at Esther's back. The shock of the sound staggered the centipedes, causing them to halt for a moment, which was enough time for Faye to dart up the steps and slash at their carapaces, slicing off segments. A centipede writhed onto the landing as it reached her. Esther shoved the point of the rod into the creature's body and coursed light down to its tip. The centipede spasmed, whipped around, trying to fix its forcipules into her flesh so it could kill her with its venom.

She stumbled back, barely avoiding its attack. Her elbow brushed against a lumpy vest pocket. *The tie.* Dragon magic had special powers in the Beyond, didn't it? She had promised to get rid of it somehow. She yanked out the tie, its length unfurling as she threw it at the centipede. Claws locked onto the fabric and drew the clothing into its mouth. A moment later the creature sizzled as if cast onto a griddle, sparked, and exploded in a burst of sound, pieces vanishing as if burned into nothing.

"I'll be damned," said Lydia.

Esther blinked, rubbing an afterimage out of her eyes.

A missile hissed out of the dark to hit Faye in the shoulder. She jerked in pain but recovered and kept slashing, cutting up centipedes in a blur of motion as the creatures kept coming. Blood began to leak through the front of her shirt.

Another crossbow bolt flew, this one missing Faye's head by inches as she ducked. Two of the ruffians hoisted a bucket on sticks and tipped it. Liquid poured onto the steps. As it oozed over the severed remains of the spasming centipedes the bodies smoked with a furious spray of acid before dissolving. Faye had to leap out of the way, then retreat as the burning liquid slopped down, step by step.

They backed into the chamber, Esther and Lydia wrestling with the door, slamming it shut the instant Faye staggered through and went down to one knee, teeth gritted, sweat pouring off her. There was no bar for the door on the inside and no way to lock the latch. While Esther hung on, Lydia set a shoulder to the apothecary's cabinet and inch by grinding inch shoved it across the floor.

The latch didn't move. No one wrenched at the door. With a final grunting effort Lydia pushed the cabinet against the door as a final if useless barrier. The good news was that the cabinet was the right height to tuck under the latch. That should stymie them for a bit.

Esther expanded her light, left Lydia by the door, and knelt beside Faye. She pulled out her earplugs. "Where's the bolt?"

"It fell out. My coat absorbed most of the force. Just give me a minute."

Esther mopped Faye's brow. "Why are you sweating so much? Did it draw blood? Let me check for poison."

With a magnificent wince, Faye peeled the coat partway down her arm and unbuttoned her shirt to expose her shoulder. The point hadn't pierced the skin, although a stunning bruise radiated outward from the point of impact where a hematoma rose, leaking.

Faye breathed through the pain, her face shining. "The sweat is the aftereffect of the accelerant spell. Didn't your last Shotgun have this?"

"No. He would vomit."

Faye gave a snort laugh as she braced herself on the ground, droplets of sweat darkening the pale stone floor before they dried and vanished. "Oh man. I won't complain ever again about flop sweats."

As Faye gritted her teeth, Esther grabbed a field dressing to contain the bleeding and helped Faye get her shirt and coat back on and buttoned up.

"Is it just me," asked Lydia, "or is it getting hot in here?"

Esther looked up the shaft of the chamber but her light didn't penetrate far. If the shaft narrowed or widened, if it reached to open air, she couldn't tell.

"Blessed Cybele protect us!" Lydia skipped back from the cabinet as the door burst into flame. The fire stalled on the cabinet, the wood bound by a protective spell. With a blast of wickedly hot air, the door dissolved into ash. A few swirls touched Esther's face as she grabbed Faye and hauled her back until they all stood with their backs to the wall, facing the empty threshold across the plinth.

No one spoke. What was there to say? She braced herself, waiting for a shower of missiles. They were sitting ducks.

A person walked into the chamber as casually as one might stroll into a coffee shop. Halting, they looked around the space and finally rested their gaze on the three humans. They themselves looked very human except for the amber eyes, four-fingered hands, folded wings, and slightly glittering skin. Esther wondered if they were the same species as the humanoid she had seen in the hoard's cages. Instead of a pair of eyelike bulges higher up on its hairless skull, this person had a pair of tentacles whose whiskery ends swept the air like sensors. They wore what Esther could only describe as a sexy jumpsuit that clung to sleek curves. Oh, to be young again. She had to appreciate the bold bitch boss look.

The right shoulder of the jumpsuit bore the trident foot of the enterprise. In their right hand the person held a whip that seemed to have a life of its own, a soft and eager hiss coming from its corded tip. Tiny eyes blinked, as if the tip was a living snout. The whip gave off a faint sickly sweet scent that tickled Esther's nose and made her tongue tingle with numbness.

In such dire circumstances, it was useful to strike first.

"Here you are at last," said Esther with an assertive smile. She had a lot of practice when it came to projecting a confidence her inner logician doubted. "Zosfadal is magnanimously ready to be quit of this unpleasantness once you agree to accept back the item he took in trade. Lydia, could you translate?"

The individual flicked the whip. Its tip snapped against the wall a foot from Lydia's head, and the Voice flinched as if spattered with drops of toxins. "No need. No deal," said Jumpsuit. "I have no further use for a crumbling old book scrawled with the unreadable ramblings of a forgotten blind poet who lived three thousand years ago."

"Homer? I'd hardly call him forgotten," said Esther. Anything to keep them talking.

"You Earthlings aren't the only ones who have poets, even if you think you are," sneered Jumpsuit. "I am here to collect the cargo we were promised."

Esther gave a theatrical sigh. "Well. It's disappointing if understandable that you lied about receiving the cargo."

"Lied?" they thundered.

The lady doth protest too much, Esther thought.

"You wouldn't want the Concilium to know your enterprise has committed multiple illegal acts of transport. How does that work? Since you couldn't file a formal claim after the entrepôt collapse, you must have denied receiving the cargo because you figured there was no evidence of receipt. Did you hope Zosfadal would settle up without checking to see if you had received the cargo? I tell you what. You need only hand over the tally stick and we will never speak of the incident again."

"You can prove nothing."

"Such a cliché is a guaranteed admission of guilt."

The wings rustled. A palpable hit!

Lydia cleared her throat. Faye straightened, panting through the last of the aftereffects. Would she be able to fight? Could they manage three against Jumpsuit and her fake Hex?

Esther kept talking. "Ah, well. If you are going to be stubborn, the Concilium will be here in a moment and their agent can sort it out."

"You're bluffing." Jumpsuit gave a command in a language Esther did not know.

"Incoming," murmured Lydia.

A pair of ruffians shoved the cabinet aside. Once the threshold was clear, three others entered carrying the two empty centipede cages, wire mesh and big enough to uncomfortably hold a crouching human. They set down the cages, mesh doors open, and spread out with their bladed weapons. The ruffian with the crossbow drew a line on Faye. Hard to miss in this situation.

Jumpsuit said, "Get in the cages."

"Are you really going up against the Concilium?"

"No need. The Concilium will never talk to you to find out. To be clear, I don't mind killing you, but my boss likes to make a profit wherever possible."

"Profit? How so?" Keep them talking.

"Skilled Hex members are much sought after."

"Hard to keep Hex members from skipping out once you send them on a mission."

"Not if they are solo replacements inside loyal Hexes who will control them." Jumpsuit glanced upward. A whistling wind could be heard, as if a Bright was moving in with all the cataclysmic change it portended. "Your choice. Live, or die."

This was a pickle. Esther felt herself running out of time-wasting options. How fast could Gus move? How long would it take for him to convince the Concilium agents? Would they come at all or would they refuse, thinking it a prank? Did people try to prank the Concilium? That would take some nerve.

She exchanged glances with Lydia and then Faye, her left hand signing *mirror*. She would reverse her light to create a barrier, but it would only be a temporary measure. Jumpsuit could set a guard and wait them out, and Esther was already tired, hungry, and thirsty.

"Where do you think our Ghost went?" she asked, hoping to spin it out a bit longer, anything to give Gus more time.

"You're bluffing." Jumpsuit signaled, and Crossbow released a bolt to smack solidly into the wall an arm's length from Faye's head. She jerked her head, as anyone would. Esther flinched as her thoughts flashed to Trey's career-ending gut wound. Who knew he had so much blood in him?

The whining of the wind grew louder. If a Bright blew through, they might have a chance to ride it out inside her mirror dome and hope the others would be forced to retreat or, at the very least, the cages would get melted into slag by the Bright's transformative field. But was that high drilling noise the wind? Or was it something else, something they did not want to be trapped with inside a small chamber?

"Holy shit," said Faye, looking up into the dark shaft. "Incoming cloud."

Jumpsuit looked up, eyes cycling to a brilliant bronze gold. Their tentacles stiffened as the whiskery ends probed the alteration in the air.

A pale shimmer descended at speed toward them, the biggest antic cloud Esther had ever seen.

Jumpsuit barked a command. The ruffians abandoned the cages and bolted for the open door.

"Sorry," said Esther, sticking her fingers into her breast pocket. "Scale it is."

"No. Don't do it." Lydia smiled like the sphinx she was or perhaps once had been, a person of many forms and many voices and many lives. "That isn't an antic cloud. Drop now, facedown."

Esther and Faye dropped. Lydia was a dangerous person with a voice like that, and anyway they were about to die or to live, and what would her dearest children think if they became orphans? Daniel had to get home, so she had to survive. She trusted Lydia.

The pitch of the whine dropped several octaves into a growl of displeasure. A crack split stones as if the force pushing against them was too much to bear. The wind returned with a gust that whipped the fragrance of a heady perfume over the hard floor and into her nose.

Pressure slid across her back, as dense and as weighty as molten ore. She was inside a furnace as liquified iron poured across her out of an unseen crucible, seeking form out of formlessness as it raced outward through the door into the landing beyond. A succession of shocked gasps was all she heard where Jumpsuit and the ruffians had run for the stairs. Their spirits were flames snapped out as the flood ate them.

A rush of air sucked past Esther. Her ears popped. A hailstorm stung her backside from head to toe, drumming on the ground around her and then ceasing, followed by a sigh like a thousand burst flowers. The tunnel smelled as sweet and rich as plumeria. A bell rang.

No, not a bell. It was a voice, harmonious and resonant.

Although the words were not so harmonious.

"You carry upon you the stench of my miscreant kin. Are you his Hex? Have you come to restore to us what we demanded he retrieve?"

Esther was so surprised by this statement that she unwisely pushed up to hands and knees without first ascertaining the speaker. Always unsound practice, yet there was a glamor at work, she felt it like butterfly kisses softening her mental spine, making her want to comply.

A person stood in the doorway, brushing long-fingered hands together as if dusting them off. The air sparkled around them with the dazzling remains of powerful magic. Wings furled inward, vanishing as their substance filled out a compact body. The individual had a handsome face, a perpendicular third eye, and skin so smooth and shining it looked polished. Their crest was modest rather than spiky, often but not always the mark of a female. The dragon lacked gills and yet Esther knew in her gut with absolute surety that this person was like to Kai, even if she wasn't sure quite what that meant. She faced a shape-shifting dragon who wore the six-petaled rosette of the Concilium as a burning gold symbol across kwos face.

17

Better to meet this peril on her feet. Esther rose, as did Faye and Lydia on either side. Strength in solidarity.

She said, "Zosfadal did not mention the Concilium was involved in this matter. He implied it was the trident foot enterprise putting pressure on him."

"These vermin have set up here as if they are rulers. On their own they do not have the authority or power to pressure an Elder One. How is it you call him? *Zosfadal*. That's a new one for him. Where does he get these names?" The dragon had a sly smirk, and Esther hoped it meant the agent would someday soon be tweaking Zosfadal's tail. But the smile turned to a simmering frown. "The trident foot's arrogance is offensive enough, but what the enterprise attempted is not only forbidden, but a defilement."

"A defilement?"

The air spun with a whirl of power as the dragon began to shift—wings appearing, body elongating, tail growing— and then, as if it realized the space was too small, the dragon settled back into humanoid form. "I know who you are, Star of Evening. Your Hex is suspended. Your presence here violates those terms. I ask myself, what would make you risk being thrown into physical prison? You must have a concern in this matter."

Not one she was going to reveal to a Concilium agent! Unless she had no choice. "Injustice must concern us all, surely. Humanoids are not allowed to traffic in dragons. So why does the Concilium allow humanoids to traffic in other humanoids?"

"So have vermin always done throughout their history. Why do you wish us to interfere when it is your own house you must clean? Regardless, your lives are not our concern. However, the Concilium must and will always be involved in matters of . . . how would you say it? A connection. A binding together."

Lydia said, "A nexus? Do you mean a nexus as a physical space, or as an object?"

The dragon waved a hand dismissively. "Neither of those. This language lacks many useful concepts but nexus works well enough. The trident foot enterprise tried to conceal their malfeasance in this regard. Even though we suspected what was going on, for a long time we could not find the evidence. So we have been waiting for their next move."

"Are you saying you've been here all along, watching the trident foot?" Esther asked.

"The Concilium must always be involved in matters of a nexus. We gained information that the trident foot were rumored to have trafficked a juvenile nexus. The evidence suggests they are part of a smuggling ring devoted to the desires of autocrats and collectors in Realms." The agent's voice grew thick with anger. "Such humanoids believe it makes them big people, as powerful as us, if they keep a young nexus and breed on them hybrid children. They treat them as prizes they can parade in front of their vermin rivals as they battle for status."

The harsh words were greeted with silence as Esther and the others grappled with what the dragon was revealing. Slavery and indenture are always terrible things. There was never any excuse for them. But of all forms of trafficking, Esther often thought that forced reproduction was the worst. To create children for the master's purpose, the master's profit, the master's pride and prestige, not because of love and shared joy.

Yet one phrase stood out: *hybrid children*.

Talk about having a concern in this matter! She had to tread with tactical care. In a case like this, it often worked to offer a statement the other person could object to and, in scrambling to object, give up more information than they intended.

"Excuse me, Respected Elder, but are you saying a nexus is not a dragon but some other sapient creature?"

"Of course a nexus is a dragon!"

"So you are a nexus?"

"Of course not!" said the agent in the tone of a person who is surprised to discover how ignorant their interlocutor is.

"But you are a shape-shifter. Isn't that a connection, a nexus, of a kind? Adapting to the appearance of other creatures and peoples?"

The agent sighed with a dramatic show of put-upon weariness. "You humanoids have neither cause nor reason to comprehend what you call dragonkind and dragon kindreds. Nor should you attempt it."

"Hold on," Faye said, her expression brightening as if a hundred light bulbs had just illuminated in her mind. "Respected Elder, are you saying a dragon nexus is called a nexus because kwo can not only shape-shift into the form of other species, as you can, but because kwo can also shift genetic markers in a way that allows kwo to breed with other dragon kindreds? And also, incidentally, other humanoid species?"

"Holy Sun Mother," murmured Lydia, looking poleaxed.

"That would explain it," said Faye with a satisfied grin, as if she had finally scratched a relentless itch. "Because Esther, didn't you tell Zosfadal that Kai couldn't be his spawn because the dragon kindreds can't interbreed? I don't know if the kindreds are different species, or genus, or if they even recognize our forms of classification. But a nexus would be an adaptation that benefited the kindreds by expanding the gene pool. I'm just riffing, here."

In Esther's gut something shifted. Something true. Some dragons could indeed shape-shift. Such dragons often acted as the Concilium's envoys and agents in the Realms precisely because they could appear to be one of the local humanoid species. Some humanoid species could also shape-shift. Even a few humans like Lydia could, although her shifting patterns took decades. Furthermore, tales as ancient as humankind told of hybrid children like the minotaur, rare, sometimes monstrous, and usually fantastically powerful.

No wonder the dragons kept this aspect of their kind a secret. A shape-shifter who can shift shapes *and* genetic markers would be precious beyond measure among the six dragon kindreds who, as Faye had aptly pointed out, apparently could not breed between kindreds. But they could, with a nexus.

"Look at me, Star of Evening," said the dragon in a voice of command.

Esther looked before she could stop herself. If only she had sunglasses.

The dragon's eyes began to shift like a kaleidoscope turning through marvelous colors and patterns. "By your expression I can see you know of what I speak. Tell me."

Kai laughing with Daniel and the extended family crowded around the big table as the little ones smeared birthday cupcake icing all over their sweet, beaming faces. Two years old. That had been ten months ago. They were almost three already.

Esther realized she was speaking out loud, recounting the memory, although she certainly had never intended to reveal any of this to the Concilium. In desperation she shut her eyes, staggering as Faye and Lydia caught her on either side. Phosphenes swirled behind her closed eyelids in an echo of the dragon's gaze.

A nexus with hybrid children.

Esther spoke without thinking, always a mistake. "I assumed that it was something all dragons could do that they didn't want us to know about."

"Is that what this one, this *Kai,* told you?"

"No. All we knew was that Kai's captors had trapped kwo in a humanoid form. But I get it now. They had to trap kwo in a shifted humanoid form if they wanted to . . ." She winced. "To reproduce with kwo. How appalling."

The dragon hissed. "Trapped by a spell. Yes, we know of this illegal magic. We feared it was the case in this regard. Otherwise kwo could have escaped. Instead, you stole the nexus."

"We *rescued* him!" snapped Esther. "I mean, I did it, not the others. I'm the one responsible. Prosecute me, if you must. I've nothing to hide. Kai asked for shelter and we gave it to kwo. We never demanded or required anything of Kai. What he and Daniel share is between them. They love each other. Or maybe you dragons don't know about love—"

"Esther," warned Lydia.

The dragon's mouth curled with displeasure. For an instant Esther was sure she looked down a smoldering gullet, but it was only the dragon speaking. "What do you hope to achieve by this disgraceful and insulting speech?"

"Do what you want with me, but leave Daniel and Kai and the family and the Hex alone! Just let them go. I'll accept the consequences."

"You will regardless. The penalty for trafficking a nexus is death."

"Fine," said Esther as her mind raced onward into the game, a form of stacking where she had to fit everything together as it fell. "But the Concilium owes it to Kai to ask Kai what kwos wishes are in the matter. Do dragons force other dragons to do their bidding?"

"We do not! How dare you insinuate we would treat our own in this manner!"

"But Zosfadal did just that—"

"Esther," warned Lydia.

The dragon was going on and hadn't heard. "We have to keep track of our genealogies because . . . never mind that . . ." The dragon had lost a little color. "It's been a long stakeout. I have revealed more than I intended."

"Sounds like tracking dragon reproduction and lineages and lost nexuses is a subject about as complicated as baseball statistics," remarked Faye.

Lydia raised a hand to forestall the rash words Esther felt rising on her tongue and herself filled the gap with a beautifully unctuous speech. "Respected One, you have my most heartfelt and profound sympathies for your exhausting task. It must be exceedingly stressful, worrying for the stolen eggs, intermittent trickles of unreliable information, constant travel only to find yourself walking up to another discouraging dead end."

The dragon sighed. "I wish I had never agreed to be assigned to this division."

Esther heard the jaded undertone and recovered her training. Create a connection, not a confrontation. "That sounds rough."

"You have no idea."

"Maybe I can help you."

A spark of suspicion kindled in the dragon's eyes. "Are you trying to wriggle out of further punishment?"

"I'm trying to do what is best for Kai. And the babies. Is it your intention to take the babies into your custody? Tear them away from the only family they've ever known?"

"Of course not!"

"It would be terrible for them to lose one of their parents. They're so young."

The dragon huffed but did not answer.

In that silence Esther saw an opening.

"Don't take my word for it. Speak to Kai." It felt as if a stone had caught in her throat as she imagined agents of the Concilium descending on the Keep and hauling away Kai. "I can't stop you anyway, can I?"

"You cannot."

"Then ask Kai if he—if kwo—lives with Daniel willingly. Reassure yourself that kwo has remained there without coercion. If you had seen Kai as I saw Kai that day, chained in this chamber, you'd know kwo was badly mistreated by the traffickers. They used cruel magic to trap a nexus in a humanoid form, and from what you've revealed, it wasn't the first time they've done such a thing. If you talk to Kai, you'll see a person who is healing, who is in a better place, who is happy. It would be barbarous and heartless to rip Kai away from all of that as kwo must have been torn away from kwos clan years ago."

The dragon steamed, but did not retort.

Esther went on. "I'm told dragons live a long time. What is a human life span to you? Why not ask Kai? Why not?"

"Do you challenge me?" The dragon fixed a swirling gaze on Esther's face, but Esther remembered to look at the dragon's tufted eyebrows, not the eyes.

"I do challenge you. I challenge you to do what is right for Kai and Daniel and the babies. I don't know what the goals of the Concilium are besides keeping trade open between Realms, but let them and their children be happy for the span allotted to them. That is not too much to ask."

"Esther," murmured Lydia, brushing her arm with a warning hand.

"What the fuck!" Marianne's voice echoed across the landing, although she was out of sight, her footfalls snapping down the stairs. "The Concilium office said we're clear to come in because there's already a dragon around here somewhere anchoring it and keeping watch . . ." She stopped dead in the threshold as the agent turned. Marianne gaped like a fish. Gus ghosted up beside her, his expression of surprise a mirror of hers.

"Hey, Mar," said Esther. "Hey, Gus. I'm just in negotiations with this agent about reassuring the Concilium that Kai is safe at the Keep with kwos chosen family."

Marianne snorted. "Only you, Esther. Only you."

The dragon's shoulders slumped with weariness. "It would be lovely to be shed of this case after five years assigned to it. Well. I make no promises. I will say only this. The life of a nexus is long, and this Kai is still young. As well, we do not desire humanoid hybrids in our clans. We are not so *heartless* or *barbarous* as to separate small fry from their progenitors. But I will need to speak to this Kai in person."

"Excellent." Esther's pulse raced, so she practiced a quick bit of calming breath. She had to be careful not to overplay her hand. "One little last detail. We can't get in the Keep without our Keeper. We need to go to Zosfadal's hoard, get Daniel, and then go to the Keep."

Lydia's eyebrows shot up.

"Ha," murmured Faye. "Bring in the heavy guns."

"Why is a Keeper at Zosfadal's hoard instead of at the Keep?" demanded the dragon.

Esther thought through all the different ways she could spin this but the agent was starting to look impatient. "To assure my compliance with his plans. I thought it was dodgy too. But I am sure Zosfadal won't try to hold on to the Keeper once *you* arrive."

"I should think not!"

"You might like to have a few words with him."

A fearfully slow and wickedly pleased smile crept across the agent's face. "Yes. I might like to have a few words with Zosfadal, the old reprobate. We've tangled before. I daresay I will enjoy this. These days it's all paperwork, paperwork, paperwork, so I don't get to say that often." The agent's form shimmered, wings swelling out so fast that Marianne and Gus jumped backward onto the dark landing. The dragon spun, shifting into a dizzying cloud. Last seen was a beautiful golden head, a long snout, and curling whiskers. "You can make your own way."

On a gust of wind, the agent flew up the shaft.

The silence stuck like cotton wool in Esther's ears, broken by the slam of Marianne's voice.

"I have to hand it to you, Esther. How you pull these things off I cannot say, but it is kind of impressive."

"Are you sure you want to transfer Hexes?"

"Damn sure. I have family to house and feed. Bills to pay."

"And expensive tastes to indulge," remarked Lydia.

Marianne gave Lydia a dry look and didn't bother to answer.

Esther pulled Zosfadal's scale from her breast pocket. "Let's go."

18

This time when the scale dissolved on Esther's tongue and she fell through the turning wheels, she was ready for the landing. She took several steps forward, touched a knee and a hand down briefly, then straightened. Her knees only gave one slight pop.

The rest of the Hex came all the way through with her. They stood on the transparent floor of the huge shell-like tower of Zosfadal's hoard. Below, the warehouse looked much the same except the workers seemed to be moving more slowly, as if wading through molasses. Instead of scurrying, the workers strolled. As one transferred a loaded hand truck to another, they paused to exchange a few words and glanced around in the way of people not sure if they are about to get in trouble. A pair of tiny sprites shared a thimble-sized glass of frothy liquid, their lanterns set on the shelf beside them.

Huh. Nothing like the frantic pace she'd witnessed when she'd arrived here before.

Instead of Shahin, an amber-eyed person with scaly skin and folded wings stood on the upward side of the ramp, holding a clipboard in one of its four-fingered hands and a walking stick in the other. After the confrontation with the trident foot lieutenant in the chamber, the sight of another of that species gave Esther such a turn that she tensed, adrenaline flooding.

Faye lowered her staff, preparing to fight. Gus drew a knife. Lydia swore under her breath. Marianne said, "Oh! The blind poet!" in a surprised tone.

"Esther Green?" said the person, evidently Zosfadal's new lieutenant.

"Yes, I am she." *The blind poet?*

"You were here before, looking for Daniel," said the lieutenant.

"I was." Years of experience traveling the Beyond had taught her to scan quickly for identifying details. The lieutenant wore a jumpsuit, loosely fitted. Instead of a pair of tentacles extruding from its upper sense organs, there were merely bulges, as if they had never developed. "Weren't you being held in the cage next to Daniel?"

"I spoke to the young man, yes. He comforted me."

"I am glad to hear it, and sorry to hear you found yourself in such circumstances that you needed comfort. A cage is no good place. May I ask to whom I am speaking?"

The person pressed a hand against their throat. Instead of a tie they wore a necklace crafted to look like a waterfall of coins. After a moment, they said, "You may call me Homer."

"Homer? Like the blind poet from Earth's history?"

The amber eyes blinked owlishly. "I am not from Earth. But I like the name, so I have taken it as a work name, if you will. No one here can pronounce my name properly."

Dealing with Shahin had given her a sense of what limitations Zosfadal put on his lieutenants. "I'm given to understand that among one of the cultures of your species there is a tradition of poetry."

"'That is correct. We cherish the treasure of verse and song.'"

"Is it true that among your species there once lived a much admired and influential poet and seer who lacked sense organs that others commonly have, so what we Earth-folk might call a blind poet?"

The lieutenant gave a gesture of assent.

She nodded and went on. "Yet, according to what I heard, most or all copies of the works of that particular poet were lost, except for a single complete opus that recently surfaced. Maybe it was traded to a boss. To Zosfadal. A one-of-a-kind jewel, if you will. You know anything about that?"

"This way." Homer turned and, leaning on the walking stick, began to ascend the ramp tap by tap.

She hurried up and offered an arm. "Do you need assistance?"

"Not with this," muttered Homer. Then added, sardonically, "If I veer toward a wall, you may redirect me."

She wanted to ask about the tentacles Homer did not have but knew it would be rude. "Your English is excellent. Did you learn it before you arrived here?"

They walked for a while up the curving ramp. She thought Homer would not answer and accepted that, like Shahin, Homer was either magically blocked from revealing certain kinds of information or too prudent to do so where the boss might listen in.

Yet as the narrowing curve brought them into sight of the entry into the apex, Homer spoke as if it had taken this long for the words to come. "I am here now, but was not before."

"I'm not sure if that's an answer or a riddle." How was it Shahin had phrased it? "Your predecessor said he came to consciousness in the hoard. His eyes, the eyes of his physical being, had never seen another place, but he knew of other places he had seen."

"Shahin is a poet, born into the palace to serve, yet I do not see him with you, though he departed in your company." A sidelong glance suggested a message, an answer, or more riddles.

They reached the apex. The vast chamber looked the same, as wide as two football fields and with its vast overhead chimney big enough to launch an intercontinental missile. The boss was curled in the center, wings furled, huge bronze head resting atop huge claws. And he was steaming. Annoyed.

A group of people stood in front of him, the gaoler among them. The wraith from the kitchen held a piece of paper in one shaking, skeletal hand. She read from it in a whispery voice as if nervous, although perhaps all wraith voices had a nervous vibrato quality.

"'We ask merely to be allowed to form a committee to examine working conditions. This committee will then recommend and request adjustments and improvements to the current code of work.'"

The boss rumbled. The hoard beneath shook as if a phalanx of heavy trucks rolled past above. "And this slowdown will only end if I allow you to form a committee? That sounds like a threat, not a negotiation. I could easily eliminate some of you. Did you think about that before you burst so rudely into my meditative sanctuary?"

"If you kill workers, that will slow down the work even more." Sshaiaia's voice quavered but she gamely went back to reading. "'Best-practice working conditions improve work outcomes. Your hoard will operate with more efficiency if the workers have more say in their operations, if they have breaks, mandated lunch, better living and leisure options, and a stake in the benefits that accrue.'"

"A stake in the benefits!" Zosfadal's crest spiked up. He raised his head, pushing up on his forelegs, wings unfurling, unfolding his massive frame. "This is a knife in my back! After all I have done! The shelter and nourishment I provide! Existence itself I have given most of you!"

Existence itself?

"This is how you repay me, with ingratitude and disloyalty!"

"What a drama queen," said Esther. As it happened, her words fell into one of those pregnant silences that occasionally overtake a large space. Everyone turned to look, so she took the bull, or in this case the dragon, by the horns and strode past the huddled group to place herself between them and the boss. "We're back."

"I have eyes and ears and whiskers! Do you think I can't perceive? Did you complete your mission?"

"We did."

"Where is my lieutenant?"

"He had other business and went on his way."

"Went on his way? What does that mean?"

"I certainly can't speak for him so he will have to explain to you. I must say, though, a committee is little enough for your workers to ask. It's not as if it would be a concession on your part. For you it is a gesture of *strength*."

"Strength," he purred. "How so?"

"They will assess the hoard's robust aspects as well as its flaws—"

"Flaws! My hoard has no flaws!"

"Really? I mean, compared to some places I've seen I guess

it's not so bad, but you could improve things around here if you wanted to elevate the status of your hoard in comparison to . . . well, you know, other places."

He lowered his head. It was like having a blazing hot pickup truck hover twenty feet from your overheated face. Rather than get caught in his eyes, Esther carefully admired the lambent scales around his muzzle. That brought her gaze close to his big, big teeth.

He spoke in an aggrieved tone. "What places have you seen? I can't risk traveling anymore."

She extended a placating hand. "I'm just saying this hoard could be a real treasury of vital culture if you instituted some changes. You're very interested in poets. A sign of good taste. Why not have poetry slams? Or recitation nights? Theatrical productions? Hire librarians to organize your collection. Get the travelers to come to you! People—even dragons!—would come from all over for, say, a festival of lost works or a fete of forgotten or little-known poets. You have everything you need here, even if I don't know how you've managed it. But I guess you're clever like that."

With a few boasting puffs of ashy steam, Zosfadal settled back into his lounging curl and groomed his whiskers, very pleased with himself. "I daresay no dragon before me ever thought about how to synthesize the last remaining expression of a humanoid mind with primordial reproductive cells that have not yet activated."

Esther was rarely at a loss for words but at least ten seconds of dead silence followed this statement.

At length she swallowed and was able to speak. "Are you saying you eat books and then give birth to them?"

"To the substance of their creative essence! But it only works if it is the last surviving, complete copy of the work in question. It took me three-quarters of my life span so far to figure that out. But *I* am still the first. *My* hoard is unique. There is nothing else like it in all the Realms, in all the Beyond. Mine. Mine. *Mine*."

"The last and the lost and the little known," she breathed. She'd heard the name Shahin before but the penny hadn't dropped until this moment. A medieval Jewish Persian poet, Shahin al-Shirazi had written, among other poems, a retelling of the story of her namesake, the famous Esther who had married a Persian king and used her influence to save her people from being slaughtered by an evil advisor.

She looked around at Sshaiaia and the others. Where on Earth did they truly come from? Given the evidence of Homer, they definitely weren't all from Earth.

Zosfadal whistled merrily as if still celebrating his triumph.

No, it was not a whistle. It was a wind swirling down the chimney-like shaft of the shell.

"Move back to the entrance by Lieutenant Homer," she said to the workers' committee. "I believe an agent of the Concilium is about to make their presence known."

Her Hex formed up around her.

A shimmering cloud of glittering gold sparks rushed into view. Zosfadal yelped. There was no other way to describe the sound. He shrank back like a cowed puppy as the cloud spun into a tornado and coalesced into a sinuously long dragon with translucent wings and golden scales. Not as huge as him but in every other way more intimidating.

Zosfadal's aggrieved huff shook the entire hoard. The workers fled, vanishing down the ramp. Only Homer stood their ground. But they were a poet, and poets are notoriously stubborn creatures wherever they may hail from.

There followed a perfect storm of tones, chimes, blurts of snappy noise, colors bright and muted, scents strong and weak, and a prickling sensation like electrical impulses that brushed at intervals against Esther's body until she thought her hair was going to stand on end, and maybe it did. The display filled the air between the two dragons, an intense and incredibly sensory dialogue that she could make neither heads nor tails of.

Even Lydia shook her head as she leaned in to whisper, "I've never met a Voice who knows this language. I've only experienced it three times, not counting today."

"Any idea?"

"The agent is doing more of the expressing with bolder and more saturated colors and stronger scents. I'm guessing the boss is getting the worst of it."

Esther checked her watch. How was Daniel doing? He'd been busy, that was clear. If she knew him, and she did, he'd opened up discussions and then stepped back to leave it to the workers to figure out. A hoard was an anomaly in terms of organizing. Many of the workers would have nowhere else to go, no Realm they could call home. Had Zosfadal really meant what he said? Were many of the people here in the hoard not "applicants" but some magical distillation of lost stories? Was that what Shahin had been trying to tell her? And what did that make him, if so?

A poet, Esther thought. Maybe that was all one needed to know.

She checked her watch three more times. Forty-eight minutes after the dialogue started, it ended with a burst of light like fireworks from the agent. Bold punctuation, that.

Zosfadal's crest flattened. His tail twitched with displeasure, and he closed his eyes with a sigh of affliction. In a rumbling whisper, which of course they all heard, he complained to himself, or to them, as if in answer to an old discussion. "She always gets what she and the Concilium want. It's so unfair."

The agent's wings shimmered, furling inward. With a twist of magic and a displacement of air and mass, the dragon became a humanoid. Brushing her hands together as if dusting off a last bit of powder, she walked over to the entrance.

"Very well. That's settled. Now you will escort me to the Kai."

"What happens to Zosfadal?"

"He has acted his part in the matter."

"Wasn't his part to traffic a dragon egg? And not just any egg, but a nexus? Didn't you deliberately intimidate me and threaten me and mine by informing me that the penalty for trafficking a nexus is death?"

"Yes, but now we know where to recover the nexus. No harm done."

At the same instant, both Gus and Lydia laid hands on Esther, Gus with a hand weighing on her shoulder and Lydia on her elbow. Only the weight and warmth of their presence stopped her from trying to punch the agent.

Her voice shook with rage. "Is Zosfadal to receive no punishment for his part in the matter? For the suffering the young one went through?"

"What's done is done. Word will spread throughout the kindreds about what the Elder One has done and how it was averted. The humiliation will be punishment enough. It's happened to him before. Why do you think he hoards here off by himself?"

Esther wondered if her ears would burn off from sheer

frustrated fury. "The usual double standard in which the powerful escape the punishment that the vulnerable suffer tenfold."

"Don't push me, Star of Evening. You and your Hex remain in violation of your suspension. A serious charge that the Concilium might be willing to reconsider, given your help with this matter. That is, *if* I ascertain the situation with the nexus to be what you claim it to be. I can still demand the most extreme punishment. So, as I said once already, let us go immediately."

Esther's mouth went dry but she managed to speak calmly. "As I said before, we need our Keeper."

"Of course."

And that was that. Now that the Concilium was involved, Zosfadal could make no objection to retrieving Daniel, and why would he? He was no longer in debt to the trident foot enterprise. He'd gotten what he wanted.

So had she. Daniel would come home. But she did not have time to absorb the relief that threatened to shake her entire body to jelly. Instead, she stiffened her resolve and, with a fake calm plastered onto her expression, rode the elevator with the agent, who insisted that Homer descend with the others via the ramp.

The kitchen was abuzz with noise and activity, only no one was prepping, cooking, or baking. Clusters of people spoke to the wraith and the gaoler and the others who had confronted the boss, all of them with hopeful, excited smiles. Daniel saw her coming. He pressed through the crowd to meet her with a big hug, then pushed back to study her.

"I can't tell by your face whether it's good news or bad news."

"You're getting out of here, so that's good. As for the rest, I don't know yet. The Concilium knows where Kai is. They're sending this agent to assess the situation. I'm wondering if this whole operation was the boss's way of getting us to take the heat for the crime he committed."

Daniel's strong hands tightened on hers. He looked past her toward the waiting agent, who was sniffing delicately at a tray of fresh rugelach. "Are they going to take Kai away?"

"She claims Kai will get a say in the matter. The babies are key. We need to go."

"Okay, okay. Okay. Let me say goodbye to everyone."

She could tell how stressed and anxious he was because it only took him half an hour to take his leave. Even as a boy he was always the last to leave a party. She wiped away tears as the anxiety, the fear, the love, the hope overflowed all in a messy stew. She had done everything she could. Knowing what she now did, she realized the family could not have kept Kai hidden forever. The matter was out of her hands.

When they reached the entry terrace, a peaceful Gloam drifted in the Beyond. They'd be able to descend immediately, thank goodness. Esther wasn't sure she'd have had the patience to endure waiting out a Bright.

Marianne halted by the clerk's desk. She pulled a folder from her pack and set papers on the desk's surface, ignoring the clerk's startled exclamation. "You've got Daniel, so you don't need me to get into the Keep. Let's sort this out now and be done."

Esther turned back. "This is really the wrong time, Mar."

"We can't go as seven anyway. The agent can't make her own way because she doesn't know where the Keep is. I'll stay behind. Just sign."

"I don't get it. How are you going to get from here to your

new and lucrative assignment . . ." She broke off. "Wait. Are you signing a contract with Zosfadal?"

Marianne's expression went rigid. She would not look Esther in the eye. "I've got expertise he's willing to pay very well for."

Esther blinked. "Are you . . . No, no, I couldn't believe that even of you. You can't have tipped off Zosfadal where Kai is."

"Is that what you think of me?"

At rare moments Esther experienced rushes of clarity, and this was one of them. But she did not want to know, not yet, not now. She grabbed a pen and scrawled her signature on all three pages. "There. Fuck you, Mar."

"You'll thank me," Marianne said.

Esther did not answer. She did not look back.

Daniel nudged her as she came up to the others. "Mom? You okay? What was that all about?"

"Let's go."

Homer gave a coin to the jester to open the gate, but the poet remained behind in the hoard as any obedient lieutenant must.

Perpetual service was his only task. But in the end, he would not bow. Shahin's words had the ring of righteous rebellion, and yet wasn't it also a description of an angel who refused to bow before Adam when commanded to do so? Maybe she would never know, even if she had given Shahin a key.

It was time to go home.

The remaining members of the Hex together with the agent descended the ramp and set foot on the Beyond. The surrounding area was currently a flat plain. In the distance, jagged mountains rose in splendor, as with the promise of adventure beyond your wildest dreams. Pillars of drifting mist wound mysterious patterns through the Gloam, like answers Esther would never learn.

"Everyone hold hands," said Daniel. It was such a Daniel thing to say. Everyone held on, and with the Keeper present Gus had just enough solidity to connect.

A Keep knows its Keeper, and a Keeper knows their Keep. The two are bound by threads of unbreakable magic, a connection to the unnamable Source, one of the strongest bonds known in all creation. Maybe only love is stronger.

A transfer wasn't instantaneous, but one could not time it because it happened outside of time. One moment they stood on the Beyond and the next they stood in front of their Keep. Its humble brick tower pleased Esther far more than the elaborate Keeps encountered elsewhere. It was like their extended family: modest, unassuming, sturdy, steadfast.

From atop the tower, behind the crenelations, six heads peered out. The wandering group had survived and they had clung to this refuge, hoping beyond hope for deliverance. Seeing them, Daniel hesitated although he clearly wanted to charge in to reach Kai first.

Lydia said, "Faye and I will talk to them."

He nodded and plunged forward, Esther at his heels. The Keep opened, and they snapped through a dry wind and a frosty veil into the waiting room of the Keep. The space was lit by a single light, everything else shadow. Daniel coughed as he sucked in a grateful gulp of the air of Oahu, rich, touched with salt, dense with the fragrance of so much vegetation and the ancient life and power of a land arisen in exactly its place in the world.

The unmistakable ratchet of a shotgun being racked broke the silence.

From the other side, past the closed curtain, a woman said firmly, *"Don't move."*

"Oh my god," said Daniel, pushing through.

The babies sat lined up in a row on the sofa, not moving, all staring raptly at the woman seated on a chair, facing them, with a shotgun in her arms. Her hair was bound up under a scarf, and she wore a long black skirt, a black long-sleeved Henley, black work boots, and a hamsah on a chain around her neck.

"Well, fuck me," she said. "Here you are."

The babies saw Daniel. "Daddy! Daddy!" they chorused, but they looked at their aunt and didn't move.

"Go on, you rascals," Chava said.

In a tumble of screaming they swarmed Daniel as he knelt to embrace them.

Chava cleared the shotgun, set it on the table, and gave her mother a kiss on the cheek and a hug. "I brought Pono over. Knew you wouldn't want that poor spoiled creature to be home alone. Howzit, Uncle," she added as Gus entered. She gave him a greeting kiss as well, then saw the agent following in his wake and looked at Esther in question.

The agent made no introduction. "Where is the nexus?"

Chava mouthed, *Nexus?*

"Kai," said Esther.

"Oh. Kai. Huh. He drove Auntie Lei to Foodland. I think she asked him to take her more to get his mind off being worried than because anyone was out of groceries." She picked her phone up from the table to call, then set it down as she cocked her head. "Nah, here he is."

From outside came the sound of wheels on gravel.

The agent said, "I'll take it from here."

Daniel jumped up, children still clinging to him.

"This is beyond your bailiwick, Keeper. Don't interfere. Don't follow me."

The agent walked out of the Keep.

Daniel set his jaw, but he did not follow.

Chava came over to him, gave him a hug, and said, "Who the fuck is that?"

Joey perked up and said, "Fuck, fuck, fuck."

"None of that," said Daniel to Joey, and to Chava, "Can you wait until they're thirteen?"

Gus said, "Lydia and Faye got the group inside. But Daniel, the Keep is still wide open and there's antic movement coming closer. The group is going to need help and direction. They were in bad shape from an antic cloud when we last saw them and who knows how long they've been waiting and if they had any food or liquid."

Daniel took several harsh breaths as he rubbed a hand over his disheveled curls. "Got it. Got it. Mom, Chava, can you . . ."

Chava punched his arm. "Yeah, we got 'em."

He followed Gus back past the curtain into the Keep's entry chamber.

As the babies swarmed Esther, planting sloppy kisses on her cheeks, Chava said, "By the way, Mom, I was just sent word an hour ago that a message came in for you. A note via a trading Hex that passed through the Plovdiv Keep."

"A message?" Esther extricated herself from the babies, who raced over to the toy shelf in a giggling mob. "What kind of message? I'm not expecting a message."

"They sent me a scan and I printed it out." Chava pulled a scrap of paper from a pocket in her skirt. She looked at it, forehead wrinkling, and got a smirk on her face.

"*What?*" Esther demanded.

"It's written in an antiquated Hebrew script. Kind of po-
etic. 'To the gracious Star of Evening . . .' I guess that's you!
'Through your eloquent kindness and peerless courage my
chains were loosened. As day always follows the dark night
so do I have hope now for a future—'"

"Let me see that!" Esther snatched the paper out of her
daughter's hand, but the script was indeed so old-fashioned
she couldn't read it because she lacked Chava's more rigorous
education.

"Mom! Are you *blushing*? You keeping something from
us? Did you find a nice Jewish boy out in the Beyond?"

"I'm going to check on Kai," said Esther in her most un-
compromising tone.

"Busted!" Chava snorted in amusement, then sobered.
"But the agent said we had to stay in here."

"Yes, I know what the agent said but I'm not leaving Kai
to face this alone. You wrangle the babies."

The paper felt as if it were burning her hand, not to mention scorching her face, but enough of this ridiculous non-
sense. She folded it up, stuck it in a vest pocket, and hustled
out the door only to discover the agent standing, as if frozen,
on the walkway beneath the sheltering canopy of the banyan. Leaves rustled, winking where sunlight from the west
poured through them. Three dogs faced the agent, block-
ing the raised path. Molasses and Babka stood with tails up,
completely silent, while Pono growled, neck tentacles pulled
in defensively.

The agent said, "What beasts are these? I believe they intend to harm me if I proceed further."

"That's their job, to guard against intruders. I'll introduce
you."

She called the dogs up one by one. To her surprise, the

agent knelt to let each dog lick her face, and then licked them in return, which was kind of gross but endearing. When introductions were completed, the dogs led the way to the back porch and around the house to the driveway turnout. Kai looked up from the car, arms full with grocery bags, looking more human than usual because he'd been to the store. His third eye popped open as he froze, staring.

"Daniel's home, no harm done," Esther said. "Where's Auntie Lei?"

"Dropped her off at her house." He stuck the grocery bags back onto the seat and took a steadying breath. "I knew you would get him back . . . ?" He stared past Esther, eyes widening.

The bell-clamor voice rang out. "This is not for your eyes, Star of Evening."

The dogs whined and dashed for cover under the house. A wind spun, rattling the branches of the surrounding trees. Something monstrously huge flowered behind her like a golden haze lifting above the roof. "Begone!"

Esther's feet moved toward the back of the house even though her brain hadn't willed them to walk. She called over her shoulder. "Kai, this agent is from the Concilium. They have tracked you down."

"What do they want with me? I'm not going home. Not after . . . I'm not going. They can't force me . . . can they?" His complexion reflected his emotion; its coppery shine dulled with fear, and he compulsively brushed his left hand over the gleaming tattooed rings on his upper right arm as he often did when he was upset.

"I have been promised they just want to ask you in person what you want to do next. To be sure you aren't being coerced. You have a choice. You get a choice."

"Go!"

The word was more threat than command. From the backyard the dogs barked frantically. Esther jogged back around the house just in time to grab Joey before the toddler could wiggle out of Chava's arms and race around to the front to see what was going on. She helped Chava wrestle the babies back into the kitchen and called in the dogs, who only stopped barking when the muffling silence of the Keep fell over them. Pono bumped her leg several times before curling up on the floor by her feet. Molasses and Babka stayed on guard at the door, growling, desperate to go outside and get into it with the intruder. But they obeyed, and the door stayed safely shut.

"I've never felt a dragon manifest on Earth! Like a bell ringing through my bones!" exclaimed Chava as they herded the babies back onto the sofa. "What the fuck, Mom!"

"I just don't know."

"Fuck, fuck, fuck," said Joey, and the other three chorused, "Fuck, fuck, fuck" in their high, chirpy, cheerful voices, and then they all collapsed into more giggling. They weren't babies anymore. They were toddlers headed for preschool and then school and then teens and Esther's heart squeezed with such infinite love for their beautiful little faces filled with mischief and promise. But she was careful not to laugh. That would just encourage them.

"Daniel would really like you to stop swearing in front of them."

"Is the Concilium going to take Kai away?"

As if in answer, a rumble like the chop of a helicopter shook the Keep to its very bones. Esther jumped up, staring at the roof. Daniel burst past the curtain and rushed out the door.

Chava turned a basilisk eye on the babies. "Go on, Mom, I've got them."

Esther went after him, the snap of transition sharp in her body. The canopy of the banyan tree whipped around, anchor roots swaying, branches clattering. The dogs cowered on the breezeway, flattened against the house. Daniel stood at the railing, hands gripping the top rail so tightly his knuckles had whitened. She came up beside him.

A copper-colored dragon hovered in place about ten feet above the backyard. Kwo was small compared to Zosfadal, with the wingspan of a Cessna, and so elegantly formed, fit for watery climes with a long body, effervescent wings, and beautifully sculptured claws tipped with shining gems. The dragon's eyes shone like jewels, and kwos crest was neither spiky and showy nor restrained and practical. A long tail swayed as if keeping the body on an even keel while testing wings after so long without them.

Wiping his eyes, Daniel whispered, "I believed Kai, you know, but it was hard to imagine it was true."

Esther had no words.

The dragon spotted Daniel at the railing. All at once, the bright and shining body twisted in on itself. In a patter of rain, Kai appeared. He ran over to the porch, bounded up, and threw arms around his love. They stood that way, embraced, oblivious to everyone around them.

Esther walked past them to find the agent, in humanoid form, standing at the base of the back porch steps.

"Well?" Esther said, heart in her throat.

The agent said, "I removed the bands. They were placed on the Kai without kwos permission. Their magic confines a dragon into a weak humanoid body. Now that the bindings are gone, no humanoid can stop kwo from departing as and when kwo wishes."

A thick emotion caught in Esther's chest. She scraped out an answer. "You are leaving it up to Kai."

"Under the circumstances of course we are leaving it up to Kai. We aren't *monsters*. Whatever you humanoids may think."

Esther opened her mouth and then closed it.

The agent gestured toward the massive banyan. "Are there many eminences like this ancient wise one here in this Realm?"

"The tree? Yes?"

The agent sighed, a scatter of sparks rising languidly from her skin. "How lovely it would be to tour the delights and pleasures and mysteries of this Realm. I've never been here. It is one of the newer ones. Don't parrots come from here? Maybe I can ask for a leave of absence. As if that will ever happen. There are probably three stacks of paperwork added to the other five stacks just since I left."

"You don't get holidays? Vacation days? Do you even measure your workday in days?"

Any answer the agent might have made was interrupted by childish shrieks of excitement. Chava, Gus, Lydia, and Faye emerged from the Keep, each with a squirming toddler in arms.

"They're kind of cute," said the agent reluctantly.

Strike while the iron is hot.

"The Concilium should revoke this Hex's suspension. You dissolved the five triangles enterprise based on our evidence of their criminal activities, which we refused to participate in. Is it illegal to refuse to participate in unlawful behavior?"

"You gave five triangles a false assurance, signed a contract, and then reneged. That is illegal."

"Had we not done so, they would still be operating, would they not? I see an opportunity for the Concilium. Reinstate the Hex. Allow us to operate under a freelance contract as we were before. When necessary, you can engage us for delicate missions regarding dragon eggs or nexuses. Missions the Concilium prefers to keep quiet. We can keep a secret. Our motive is not profit, and it isn't self-gratification."

"Altruism can be a form of gratification, but I take your point. For example, we have had little success in tracking down the source of the spell that confined your Kai to a humanoid form. The existence of such a spell presents a troublesome threat."

"The offer is open. My Hex is eager to get back to what we do best."

The agent arched a skeptical eyebrow. "The Beyond and the Realms are many. You are just one Hex. What you accomplish is merely a drop here and there in a vast ocean."

"It makes a difference to that drop," said Esther. "One starfish at a time."

"What is a starfish?"

"I'd be happy to show you. If you can get leave for a visit to Earth. In fact, I have some questions about the Concilium not including leave or holidays as part of your contract."

"Do you never stop with these entreaties and petitions?"

"Who knows, perhaps you have come to the place you are now for just such a time as this. Can you stay for supper?"

"You don't even know me," said the agent.

They watched as the others entered the house hugging, chattering, and laughing with the relief people feel when they have reached their desired destination after a dangerous journey.

Grant us grace, kindness, and mercy.

"Yet if it pleases you," Esther said, "you would be welcome."

The last rays of the setting sun gilded the banyan tree in glory, the light splitting off its massive shadow to make it seem as if it were two trees, not one. In the darkening sky the evening star shone alongside a crescent moon. Wind stirred in the trees. A gecko chirped. Pono stuck his head out the door and barked once, interrogatively, wondering if they meant to come in.

"Maybe I will," said the agent rebelliously.

With a smile, Esther led her inside.

ACKNOWLEDGMENTS

I send my most effusive thanks to my beta readers, local consultants, and general support crew: Cheri Kamei, Emma Mieko Candon, Krystle Yanagihara, Bogi Takács, Akiko Chang, Naci Hirayama, Melanie Ujimori, Rhiannon Rasmussen, David Rasmussen-Silverstein, Alexander Rasmussen-Silverstein, Aliette de Bodard, Malinda Lo, Cindy Pon, Vida Cruz, Victor Ocampo, and Zen Cho.

As always, my heartfelt thanks to the stellar team at Tordotcom Publishing: my still most excellent editor Lee Harris; tireless and efficient editorial assistant Matt Rusin; copy editor Christina MacDonald; proofreader Norma Hoffman; production manager Jacqueline Huber-Rodriguez; production editor Jeff LaSala; designer Greg Collins; jacket designer Christine Foltzer; ad/promo designer Angie Rao; the ace marketing team of Becky Yeager, Renata Sweeney, Sam Friedlander, and Michael Dudding; the indefatigable publicists Caroline Perny, Saraciea Fennell, and Jocelyn Bright; and of course publisher Irene Gallo. Special shout-out to Emmanuel Shiu for the spectacularly perfect cover illustration.

For further reading, for anyone interested in the historical Shāhīn, I recommend *In Queen Esther's Garden: An Anthology of Judeo-Persian Literature,* translated and with an introduction and notes by Vera Basch Moreen, Yale University Press.